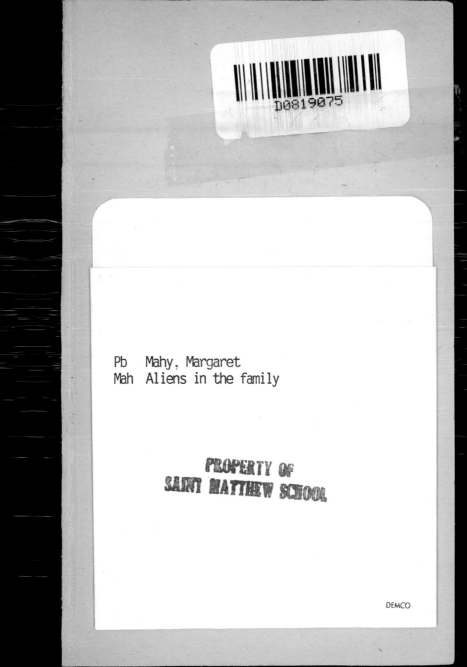

D0819075

Pb   Mahy, Margaret
Mah   Aliens in the family

DEMCO

ALSO BY MARGARET MAHY

THE CATALOGUE OF THE UNIVERSE
THE CHANGEOVER: A SUPERNATURAL ROMANCE
THE HAUNTING

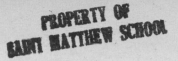

ALIENS
IN THE FAMILY

MARGARET MAHY

AN
APPLE
PAPERBACK

SCHOLASTIC INC.
New York Toronto London Auckland Sydney

ISBN 0-590-40321-4

12 11 10 9 8 7 6 5 4 3 2 1   4   7 8 9/8 0 1 2/9

Printed in the U.S.A.   01

ALIENS
IN THE FAMILY

Contents

Part One

Part Two

Part One

Introduction

Even the most ordinary of days can be full of secrets and mysteries, and this particular Thursday was no exception. It was full of people setting off from certain places and arriving at others. Thursday's children have far to go . . .

Jacqueline Raven was not only travelling on a Thursday, she had been born on a Thursday too. She was setting out from a small country airport to visit her father whom she had not seen for over a year. Since she last saw him he had married again and now had a new family that Jacqueline had never met. Her own life had changed too, so much so in fact that she found it hard to believe that the girl she had once been had ever existed.

She was sure the new family would not like her and was quite certain that she would not like them but there was no way around it. If she wanted to see her father again she would have to see them too, for the new children belonged to him more than she did these days, and she must try hard to accept them and like them. Not that this was her only problem. She did not feel at all comfortable about leaving Pet, her mother.

"Don't forget," she said, turning anxiously to Pet, "if Granny can't sleep and starts getting up in the night and tidying drawers, that little blue pill is the one to give her. It just makes her restful and —"

"Don't worry, dear!"said Pet. "I won't forget." But Jacqueline, who really preferred to be called Jake, knew her mother often did forget such things, and although she was always sorry afterwards, afterwards was usually too late.

"Flight 317 to Christchurch is boarding now at Gate Two," announced the girl at the departure desk. It was such a small airport that you could hear her natural voice as well as the magnified one coming over the public address system. She was her own echo.

"Oh dear," said Pet. "I do wish you weren't going. You will come back won't you? I mean, you won't get too enchanted by lovely old David and his lovely new family. No — that's not fair of me. But you *will* come back?"

"Of course," Jake reassured her. "It's just a holiday." They hugged each other awkwardly.

"Give him a hug from me too," said Pet, not needing to say who 'him' was but they both knew that Jake found it hard enough to give hugs on her own behalf. She could not pass one on. People were beginning to drift out across the tarmac towards the plane but still Jake hesitated. She wanted to go — and she wanted to stay.

"Dear, please don't worry!" Pet exclaimed. "Anyone would think you were the mother, not me! Just you go ahead and have a wonderful time."

2

Jake strode determinedly out of the air terminal looking rather like the hero of a cowboy movie striding towards a confrontation with the bad-guys in the main street of town.

★　　★　　★

While Jake was saying goodbye to her mother, and in the city far away her new relations were arguing about the sort of thing that might make her feel at home, a farewell of a very different sort was about to take place in a different space and time from her own.

Bond was walking confidently along the rounded corridor of his School – the only home he had ever known. He was the only one awake in the dormitory and the dreams of his fellow students fretted the edge of his thoughts like a cloud of rainbow gnats, staining his vision with their colours. It was the first time he had experienced such quietude and he was able to hear the hum and groan of the School as it skipped through space like a stone skipping over the surface of a pool.

His School could flick through the dimensions of space as easily as a cat takes short cuts through back gardens. It could swing around whole planetary systems gathering in enough of their energy to hurl itself outwards on vast journeys, not only through space but back in time as well.

As Bond walked, a blue light moved with him matching his pace exactly.

"Nexus ahead," said a soft, mechanical voice. Bond hesitated for a moment and the light hesitated too. "Your final interview before assessment!" Bond still held back, and after a moment the light moved on without him. He had to hurry to catch it up.

Ahead, another light brightened to form a reassuring, rosy cone, blushing warmly in the dark. The light was falling on the nexus, a chair set where the light bled a little into the surrounding dark at the junction of two rooms. The floor curved up into the shadows, for there was no gravity to make an 'up' and a 'down', or any real direction at all.

The rooms were linked in front of the chair by screens beaded with coloured dials. Bright worms of light looped along through them, rising and falling to make a pattern Bond was unable to decipher. In other small windows, numbers, symbols and diagrams flickered, briefly flashing their secrets before disappearing into electric night.

As Bond sat down, one of the screens lit up with a pattern of shifting bands confirming what he had already been told. He was to take his first test and had been awakened and called by his teacher, the voice of the School itself – that energetic and courageous School which moved continually among the stars. Its pupils, the young Galgonqua, would each be called upon at some stage to carry out their task of adding to the great Inventory.

"Well, Bond," said a musical voice, "you are about to set out on your first test. If you succeed you'll become a probationer and interface with the Inventory. Now, give me an account, in your own words, of where we are and what you are to do."

"We've come back through hypothetical time to actual time by tachyon transference," recited Bond promptly. "We're back in the past at some time prior to the Exodus, and we're lined up with a small city on the old, original planet which the prophetic circuits have predicted will provide us with good information for the Inventory. One of the probationers," he hesitated, "my sister Solita, is currently interfaced with the Inventory and her personality component is invested in a very simple Companion which has been concealed in the city below." He broke off suddenly. "I've never worked with a Companion before," he said looking at the screen as though it was a face. "It'll seem very strange to have Solita talking to me out of a machine."

"Yes, it will seem strange," agreed the teacher. "In some ways you may feel more alone *with* the Companion than you would feel without it, but part of the test is intended to measure your strength in this way. Go on."

"Well," Bond spoke with increasing confidence, "using students' access to the Inventory, I'm to design an appearance that will blend in with the time and the place. Then I will transform, go down amongst the ancestors and try to locate the hidden companion by unravelling its electronic trace. Once I find it I am to take it out of the city to one of the given places where my temporary body will be dissolved and the companion and I will then be transported back to the school."

"And . . . ?" encouraged the voice, as Bond stopped.

"Oh yes, of course! I'm to record continually. I have to notice everything."

"Does it all sound very difficult?" sang the voice.

"I don't want to seem too confident," said Bond smiling modestly as he spoke, "however — no, it doesn't sound too hard. I know the images, I take false memories well and I enjoy untangling electronic traces. I love the challenge of it."

There was a subtle change in the pattern on the screen but Bond did not know what the change might mean. "How do you think you will maintain a temporary appearance?" asked the teacher. "It could be embarrassing to find yourself drifting back to your true shape in a strange city. It may be funny when you're in class — some of the hybrids produced by involuntary reversion are certainly entertaining — but out among the ancestors . . . " The sentence was left unfinished, and Bond dropped his head onto his chest.

"You know I'm not good at that," he sighed. He felt, soft as a breath on his cheek, the first touch of a feeling that he did not recognize, for he had had very little reason to feel it before. It was doubt — the forerunner of fear. He knew he must not let it show. He began counting to himself and repeated a formula that filled him with a peaceful feeling. His alarm did not vanish completely but he sensed the power of acceptance, and all time (his own time, hypothetical time and the past time he was about to explore) became a simple succession of small, rich minutes through which he could travel quite happily.

"Very good!" said the teacher approvingly. "Note that your hands are still tense, however. It could cause fumbling at a vital moment."

Bond looked down at his hands and saw with surprise that his double-jointed thumbs were interlocked so tightly that it looked as though he had tied them in a knot. He took a deep breath and watched as they relaxed. His gill flaps, which had bleached away and become almost invisible, coloured up again, looking like black and scarlet lace tattooed onto his skin between the base of his ears and his throat.

"After all," the teacher observed, "there is no point in a test unless it tests something. My last advice is this. Take nothing at face value."

"'Suspect all appearance'," quoted Bond. It was a primary instruction taught to all Galgonqua.

"You must now go to your first assessment. When you have drawn up a specification, present it to the students' Inventory. You will understand that we won't let you go down unless we feel you have chosen a reasonable form."

"But I can make myself look like a hero, can't I?" asked Bond, looking up and laughing. "Every little bit helps! Oh — and may I wear my old stone?" He was talking about an ancient sliver of jade, a birth present from his unknown father.

Children of the Galgonqua did not know their parents. They were loved and nurtured by the School. "It came from the old planet in the beginning," he said. "That's been proven. It's a good luck stone."

The teacher considered this and did not reply at once. Finally he said, "No matter how remote it seems we must always consider the possibility of an object anomaly. If it was to encounter itself in an earlier form for example, it could set up a field that would stun you, or cause your own stone to vanish, or more seriously, it could disrupt your change. As you find it hard to maintain a metamorphic form you might begin dissolving if you were wearing that stone and found yourself near the rock from which it was originally quarried. And it's known that such objects try to equalize the time pressure by unifying. They pull together and can affect probability." He paused. "On the other hand, since we have faith in the prophets, even if we don't understand how they work, we are encouraged to consult good luck signs too. And if your stone came from there in the beginning, the anomaly would at least be local. If assessment clears it and the prophecy read-out is favourable, you may wear your stone. Now – on your way, Bond, and good luck with your test."

The pattern of lights was abruptly extinguished. Alone once more, there was nothing left for Bond to do but to get up from his chair and walk off through the halls of the school. As he walked, an aura of light moved with him.

* ★ ★

On the planet below, but even further back in time, a man by the name of Sebastian Webster was setting out on the return journey to his home village. Suddenly he put his hand to his ear as if he had been stung. The landowner, eyeing him reproachfully, did not notice.

"I didn't think *you'd* walk out on me," he was saying. "Look at the work that still has to be done! We could use another pair of hands. The Maori boys – well, I can't say I'm surprised about them moving on – but you're an Englishman! I can help you build a wee cottage here, you could find yourself a bride and probably get some land of your own someday. I mean . . . " he gestured widely, "look around you! It's all there for the taking! It doesn't belong to anyone. Your son could be a gentleman. Mine will be!"

"I have a wife already – and a son," Sebastian replied, smiling politely, aware of the scrutiny of his Maori friends. He had walked over the peninsular with them to do a few days' work in return for some blankets and tobacco, and was now about to accompany them back through the bush-covered hills.

"Yeah, well – you look the part," said the landowner scornfully. Sebastian wore his long, fair hair twisted up in a knot Maori-style, and a long, greenstone pendant hung from his ear. He nodded, not bothering to try and explain how he felt to this *pakeha* – he no longer considered himself one.

Sebastian had at last found a life he loved. The whaling-boat that had brought him to this country now seemed like a distant nightmare.

He set off with his friends towards home, leaving to others the clearing of the bush, the pit-sawing of timber and the planting of crops. They began their climb up the vast slopes of an extinct volcano, a great shell, one side of which now opened into the sea forming a safe harbour for ships. They moved easily even on the steepest parts for they were accustomed to their land of hills and bush.

"Your *tautau*," said Hakiaha, touching his own earring. "I saw you raise your hand to it. Did it warn you, *Wehipa?*" He addressed Sebastian using the Maori form of 'Webster'.

"It stung me and then it felt as if it weighed a little heavier," replied Sebastian. He was proud of his greenstone earring which was a rare present. Wearing it, he was a part of the life of his chosen village or *pa*, and belonged with his friends and his wife, whom he loved. All the same, he understood the changes taking place on the peninsular in a way that Hakiaha did not. Sebastian understood fences. At that moment the stone tugged him again and he felt a slight pause in things, as though the world had suddenly become unreal for a moment. Even the stone felt insubstantial – temporary – as if it might melt like ice and run in green tears down his neck and vanish.

"*E hoa Wehipa!*" said Koro, his other friend. "It's only a little ghost. Everyone knows that there's a ghost in that *tautau,* but we didn't think it would hurt a *pakeha*. They don't see ghosts."

The burning and tugging faded, but his ear began itching. "The ghost might be calling your name," suggested Hakiaha, as they resumed their journey. And for a while, Sebastian was able to forget the stone and the ghost which had taken him by the ear trying to turn him in a certain direction or even to warn him of something.

1. The Alien

"Dora! They'll be here soon!" Dora's mother, Philippa, banged impatiently on the bathroom door. "What on earth are you doing in there? Anyone would think you were hiding from Jacqueline instead of being pleased that she's finally coming to see us."

Dora's younger brother, Lewis, lay on the floor with felt pens scattered all about him, drawing a wonderful, soaring eagle. Its wings spread from one side of the page to the other. He looked up at his mother curiously.

"Are we *really* pleased to see Jacqueline, or just pretending?" he asked. "There's no room for her really, is there?" He knew they had managed to buy their new house cheaply because it was so small. ('A two-bedroomed house,' the real estate agent had said, 'but the sunporch can be used as an extra bedroom.') Lewis slept in the sunporch.

"Dora's room is a double one," said Philippa quickly, but she was troubled too. "We'll add on to the house next year," she continued, rather more as if she was reassuring herself than justifying anything to Lewis, "but we can't wait a year before we meet Jacqueline, can we?"

Lewis sighed and went back to drawing his eagle. Sometimes he thought he might actually draw himself right into one of his eagles and fly off into a sky on the other side of the paper. He had the feeling that all was not going to be as they expected, and he was sick of surprises because his life had held so many in the last few years. The first surprise had been when his own father suddenly vanished from home, then came back not as a father but as a visitor. He had been surprised again twelve months later when David had started calling on them, bringing presents and flowers. He had been astonished when his mother married again, astounded by the trip to Australia (which followed immediately because David was transferred to his firm's Sydney office for a term) and now, a year later, he was amazed to find himself living in a house where everything was new – nothing scratched, nothing dented, curtains, carpet and kitchen all clean and bright. He sometimes felt as if he and his family were not real, that they were living a television commercial instead of true life. What with so many surprises coming so quickly after one another, all Lewis wanted to do now was to work out how to grow unsurprised again. The arrival of a new sister to share such a small space would be no help at all.

"Are we really and truly glad she's coming?" he asked again.

"Of course we're glad!" Philippa stated indignantly. "David's longing to see his little girl again."

13

"Not little! She's twelve!" complained the eight-year-old Lewis, for now there would be two of them . . . not only another sister, but another *older* sister to tell him what to do and what not to do.

"Gosh, I know how I'd feel if I had to spend a year without seeing you," Philippa cried. She fell onto her knees beside her son and tickled him so that his hand jumped a little while he drew his eagle's eye, making it look very cheerful when he had meant to make it look fierce. Suddenly it all became too much for Lewis.

"Don't! Don't! Stop it!" he screamed, rolling, laughing and kicking wildly, but when his mother stopped tickling he looked at her solemnly. "*You* wouldn't let anyone else have us, would you?" he demanded, sounding confident but feeling a little worried too, as he thought she just might.

"Jacqueline has been with her mother," Philippa said rather sharply as if Lewis had criticized David for letting his daughter go. "That isn't just anyone, now is it?"

"Mothers always keep the children – they're the lucky ones," said Lewis, rolling back onto his stomach and resuming work on his eagle.

On David's chest of drawers in the master bedroom stood a photograph of a round-faced girl with long, brown hair and blue eyes looking shyly at the camera – mysterious Jacqueline, the missing piece of the jigsaw puzzle family. Once a week her letters arrived with messages written all over them.

D. RAVEN ONLY! DEADLY SECRET or WATCH OUT FOR SPIDERS! THIS LETTER HAS A POISONOUS STAMP! Once she drew a skull and crossbones as if her letter was a pirate flag. Once she drew a dagger dripping with blood.

It certainly made collecting the mail seem very adventurous, and when the letters were propped up against the clock waiting for David to come home and read them, they looked out of place but exciting and dangerous in the brand new, crisp, clean house.

Meanwhile, in the bathroom with a chair pushed under the door handle to jam it closed, Dora was trying out smiles in the mirror, practising to be beautiful. She had practised and practised for a year, but so far nothing much had happened. Of course, once her braces were taken off her teeth she knew she would have a fascinating smile. In the meantime she had decided to concentrate on getting her hair right. Hidden away in the drawers of her dressing table were numerous bottles of hair dye. Though she had never dared to use it, Dora enjoyed reading the labels and imagining herself as 'Golden Glow' or 'Kiss of Fire'. But for now she had fair, bubbly curls – not bad, except for being a bit straggly around the bottom.

"I look as if I'm coming unravelled," she had complained at breakfast.

"I like you the way you are," said Philippa, "and so does David."

Of course Dora knew parents had to say things like that, yet she felt certain that at any moment now, a door would open somewhere, almost accidentally, and some wonderful person would be on the other side looking for a girl just like her. She tried to be prepared for this meeting at all times. Walking down the street she would study the people coming towards her, wondering *Is this the one? Will this boy look at me and love me forever? Will this woman see me and stop in her tracks, crying 'That's the very face for my new movie!' or '... to advertise our wonderful hair shampoo!'* So working away in the bathroom, Dora smiled energetically and hastily tried on various clothes, determined to look her very best, wanting Jacqueline to like her, but not to feel better than her, nor to be any prettier.

At first she scarcely heard the rich, purring sound out in the driveway as David's car – the family's 'best' car – returned from its trip to the airport. Then she suddenly grew still with a smile of greeting fixed on her face as if it had been sprayed on. It was too late to do anything more. Anyhow she was as good as she possibly could be.

"Oh gosh, I'm nervous," said Philippa. "Should I run out and – no, I'll wait here and look easy-going. Get up on your feet, Lewis."

"What about Dora?" Lewis whined. "She won't come out of the bathroom."

"Wrong, wrong, wrong, Mr Smarty! Here I am!" cried Dora as she launched herself into the living room. You had to be careful how you looked at Dora, Lewis always thought, because if you looked at her in the wrong way she would sometimes burst into tears and slam doors. Still, it was hard to be sure of having the right expression on one's face when she came at you without warning, as she did now, wearing black jeans and a tight black jersey with sparkling bits all over it. Somehow this accentuated the glittering braces on her teeth which was a little unfortunate. The neckline plunged low on her chest but there was nothing much to stop it. A smooth teardrop of greenstone hung at the base of her neck on a silver chain. Although she was not wearing lipstick, knowing full well that Philippa would send her back to wipe it off again, Dora had certainly darkened her eyebrows and made her eyelids and lips shiny with a touch of Vaseline.

"You look very nice, Dora," said Philippa diplomatically, not daring to criticize in case she started a scene. It wouldn't look good with Jacqueline about to walk through the door. "Don't you think your blue shirt would've looked better though? A jersey looks so hot on an afternoon like this." They heard footsteps on the concrete path leading up from the garage.

"It's got a low neck," Dora babbled nervously, stroking the front with a loving hand, making the mother-of-pearl sequins ripple and shine. "Isn't it good value? I got it at the op' shop with my Christmas money. It was really cheap because it was such a small size. I'm very petite."

The front door opened and David came in first carrying a small, faded pack. He was a short, quick man with teasing sad eyes like a clever monkey, but at that moment he looked incredulous and alarmed. He was followed by a tall, lanky creature wearing old blue jeans, a fringed suede jacket and a cowboy hat. Bright, stern eyes barely showed beneath the wide brim. David's Jacqueline came into the room like the Lone Ranger bursting in on a shifty group of cattle rustlers.

"Well, folks, here she is at last," exclaimed David. "My little Jacqueline." He glanced quickly at Philippa who bounded anxiously forward.

"Jacqueline – it's lovely to meet you at last." She hesitated then went to hug the cowboy. The cowboy held out a scratched brown hand with such a firm movement that Philippa had to change her mind and shake hands instead.

"Jackie, darling!" said David. "Don't be such a silly girl," and setting a good example he enveloped her in a big hug which she received stiffly.

"Call me Jake," she said to her father. "I told you in the car – that's what I'm called now. Jake."

To Dora, Jake appeared as foreign as if she really was a cowboy or something even stranger. She looked like an alien in the new house – a fierce Jake from outer space, there in the family sitting room.

2. The Lone Ranger from Outer Space

So Dora realized that she had offered to share her bedroom with a creature of another species. It was not a nice thought. She had looked forward to sharing with long-haired Jacqueline because she hadn't made any close friends at school yet, and she loved friends. She had chosen to believe the shy photograph rather than the envelopes dripping with bloody ink, and had imagined she might take Jacqueline under her wing and teach her to do her hair in some pretty way – perhaps the sort of braid that the girls at school called a french plait. You could share a bedroom with someone who would enjoy learning to do their hair in a new way. But the Lone Ranger – even without a horse – was another matter altogether.

Meanwhile, Lewis was thinking things had turned out better than he would have believed they could. He studied Jake from a distance with new interest, trying to work out what the cowboy hat might really indicate.

"It's wonderful to have you here with us," David said, holding Jake's hand for a moment. It lay in his large hand like some small wild creature pretending to be dead so it would be set free again.

David looked at her with uncertainty. "We're almost settled in now. As you can see, the house is a bit like a caravan – very tiny."

"We got it cheaply because it was so small," Philippa explained nervously, and added, as she always added, "We'll build on to it in a year or two. How about something to eat? Did you have anything on the plane? Once you've had a cup of tea and some cake a place always seems more like home."

Jake nodded but said nothing. It was hard to judge her expression in the shadow of her hat.

"So let's have a good look at you." David reached out and firmly removed the cowboy hat from her head. Lewis held his breath, thinking Jake might whip out a six-shooter and force David to give it back. Jake did no such thing however, and Lewis saw clearly that she was just as helpless as he was, even if she was much taller. Dora stared in dismay. Jake's hair was cut as short as Lewis's. It was mousey brown and looked as if it had actually been nibbled off by mice while its owner slept.

Nits! thought Dora. *She must have had nits!* She almost melted away in horror. She then thought of the wall behind her bed in the room Jake was to share, pinned all over with pictures of Brooke Shields and other beautiful girls. Dora half imagined these pictures would work on her like good spells while she was asleep so that when she awoke she would have grown to look a little more like them, but she saw at once that such pictures might actually seem insulting to someone with nibbled hair. And then she wondered miserably how you could tell immediately that someone was a declared enemy without them even saying a word. The long-haired, shy Jacqueline in the photograph could have been a friend. But this Jake could be nothing but a foe.

Dora shifted her gaze from Jake to her pack. It was very small and very battered. It was unexpectedly pathetic. There was nothing sinister about it, but nothing nice either. No-one had lovingly packed it; no-one had gone to the trouble of ironing clothes for her to take away, or had worried about what a new, strange family might think of the way she dressed. Dora could tell all that from just the outside of the pack.

"Is this all you have?" Philippa asked, astounded.

"I don't need much," replied Jake calmly. "Did you think I'd have a lot?" she said with a sudden smile. "I've got – you know – la la la . . . " She made a wavy gesture with her hand.

"And what does 'la la la' stand for, may I ask?" said David a little grimly.

"Right now it stands for clean pants, a toothbrush, a spare pair of jeans, a pair of sneakers, a book of horror stories." Jake shrugged. "It generally stands for lists of things not worth telling about."

Dora's heart missed a beat. She detested stories about monsters, vampires, ghosts, murderers and great battles between the forces of good and evil. She hated science fiction. What she enjoyed were ballet books about girls dancing beautifully in rose pink dresses or homely, comfortable stories, and, though she did not tell anyone, she still enjoyed reading her old copies of Milly Molly Mandy. Horror stories on the other hand, filled her with dread, not because she actually believed in were-wolves and vampires, but because the stories always suggested some unnamed thing, huge and hairy, moving through the darkness. Now she looked at Jake with despair. Jake smiled with one side of her mouth and not the other which looked more like a sneer. Picking up her pack, Jake hoisted it onto her shoulder with a movement that was easy but at the same time seemed resigned.

"Let me carry that for you," suggested David. "Come on, Jackie, don't be difficult."

"It's not heavy," she argued. "Anyhow, I'm used to carrying my own heavy things."

David took it from her all the same. "You're sharing – you've got to share – " he paused, "Dora's room."

Jake looked at Dora. "Right on!" she said quietly, unsmiling, and followed David. She might as well have said "That's the end! That's the absolute *pits!*"

"Mum," whispered Dora as the door closed behind Jake and her father, "I hate her."

"Don't be silly," Philippa whispered back. "Of course you don't. You can't! But – oh dear – she certainly is different from what David said she was like."

"He said she could ride horses. That all she thought about was horses. I thought she'd be the sort of person who wore a silk shirt and jodhpurs – a real rider," muttered Dora.

"I thought David was being too confident," commented Philippa. "He wanted to believe things would be straightforward. Never mind! We'll manage."

"How long is she staying?" asked Dora.

"Not long! Well – just until the end of the school holidays." Philippa spoke in a subdued voice.

"That's ages. I think I might be glad to go back to school again, even though I am going to be in Mrs Winward's class!"

"Give her a chance, poor girl!" exclaimed Philippa. "In a day or two she'll probably be like one of us."

But Dora thought that families were like planets. Each had its own creatures breathing its own special air, and no-one as alien as Jake could ever live happily on their particular planet.

3. Space Invaders

Gliding slowly down the street, Bond looked so bright and energetic that some people smiled to see him go by while others frowned, mistrusting his roller skates on a busy city footpath, or puzzled by his suit of many pockets. Pockets of orange, green and gold, all differently shaped, were sewn down the legs of his blue jeans, and there were others like bright windows on his brown shirt. He was still dazed by his surroundings, for although he had been given what the Galgonqua called 'false' or 'induced' memories which enabled him to recognize and understand the uses of things he had never seen before, it did not altogether take the surprise out of those things. *That's a bicycle!* thought Bond, amazed, for it seemed to him that the pedalling motion of the rider was winding up invisible thread from the road behind him.

As he skated weaving along the street, Bond was performing two functions – both part of his test. He was receiving all sorts of signals, but was trying to untangle one in particular – the faint, unconscious trace emitted by the 'missing' Companion. It was also part of the talent of the Galgonqua that they should record. So Bond looked at things differently from anyone else in the street — for he looked at everything twice. His first glance was the surprised one, and his second was the remembering one. He chose to remember the most ordinary things: empty Coca-Cola cans in the gutter, the ill-shaven old man selling lottery tickets and horse-racing news, people's cars, shoes, shorts, shirts, the chains around their necks, the rings on their fingers. Their faces interested him too but he didn't dare look at them long, in case they noticed his curiosity and studied him too closely.

He skated along, smiling as he went. Sometimes he would see something not included in his false memory file and then he would blink as if his mind was taking a photograph. Later, if he was successful, these details would be read off by the School and recorded in the gigantic Inventory of the Galgonqua which was eventually intended to hold all the information, feelings, memories, sensations, ideas, jokes, riddles, mysteries, answers and explanations in the entire universe. They had already been building it up for thousands of years but sometimes it seemed as if they had barely begun.

Though Bond drifted through the crowds without any apparent purpose, he was in fact following his clue. The faint impulse from the Companion was a thread he could follow, running through his head, a constant drone like the humming of a tiny fly, and growing more distinct when he turned his face to it — a thrill which he alone in the busy street could pick out of the air. Earlier in the day this sensation had been interrupted by distance, by his own confusion, by pneumatic drills, by the radios of taxis calling to each other across the city like animals separated from their herd, and even by the electronic presence of microwave ovens in restaurants and coffee bars. He had patiently picked his way through all this, untangling that one thread from all the threads the city offered him. But now it was constant. He had trapped it inside him and even began to feel his old confidence returning.

It's not a difficult test after all, he thought, *or perhaps it is – for others.* He had always been very clever at detecting and unravelling the signals by which the Galgonqua kept in touch with one another. He was a tireless and deft unraveller. So at last, by following this impulse and recording as he went, he came to a particular shop and stood outside it, hesitant and uncertain.

Peering in the door as a cautious animal might inspect a trap, Bond saw racks of old cardigans and dresses, somehow more sinister than new ones as if ghosts had been trapped and strung up on coat-hangers. Even from the door it seemed to Bond that the brown jersey on the front of the rack still carried the shape of the woman who had once worn it. He went in at last, feeling his skates, so quick and clever out on the footpath, grow clumsy and heavy on the worn, green matting. A woman sat knitting behind the counter.

"Can I help you, dear?" she asked.

"Just looking," replied Bond, and he *did* look with great curiosity at vases, china ornaments and old cups and saucers set on a shelf. On other shelves behind the woman were the more valuable things, including a black box studded with buttons and little dials. Bond knew at once that this was no ordinary transistor radio. This was what he was searching for – the Companion emitting its constant location call but giving no information about what had happened or why it was here in this shop or quite how he was to get it. He supposed it must be for sale and he had been issued with money but had he been given enough? He felt frightened at the sight of the box, so square and dark in the shop full of ghosts. It seemed so open, so obvious, yet he was sure there must be a catch.

All the time he hesitated he was aware that in that black square, under those studs and dials was unbelievably tiny and intricate machinery, and that set in a maze of pinpoint circuits was the voice, the reasoning and some of the powers of his older sister Solita. She had been sent down in this form to be part of his test, and also to record for the Inventory in a different and more complicated way than a young, untested student such as Bond could manage. The Solita in the box had been set in a state of unconsciousness but the School had told him that her brother's voice was one that might interrupt whatever strange mechanical dreams she was dreaming. He was to reclaim her, awaken her and bring her home.

At that moment the woman behind the counter spoke to him once more. "Can I help you, dear?" she asked with the identical words and expression she had used a moment ago.

"How much is the transistor?" Bond enquired casually. His blood chilled as the woman calmly pulled the knitting off her needles and rose, pointing them at his heart like twin swords. They were steel and very sharp.

"You must be the one," she said in a high, cold voice. Simultaneously, the curtains around the changing booth behind Bond were swept aside and a dark figure appeared – a man with white hair erupting around his forehead and chin as though he were more goat than man. His bumpy forehead even looked as though it might be growing horns, and his yellow eyes bulged.

"You!" the man snorted. "Did you not think there might be a trap for anyone the School sent down? Your people are not all-powerful, you know."

"Who are you?" Bond asked, appalled at being recognized, but even as he spoke, the answer – incredible and terrifying – came into his mind. Under the skin of his wrist throbbed a mechanism called 'the pulse' which enabled the School to trace his progress even though he could not contact the School. Contact until the proper time was strictly forbidden. He touched the pulse with his thumb.

"You're Wirdegen!" he cried. "You're trying to find a way into our Inventory!"

"Knowledge is the greatest treasure of all," said the man. "The woman there – she's nothing. She's under our control, as you will be in a minute."

Bond quickly turned and shouted across the counter to the Companion "Wake up, Solita! Wake up!"

"You can't wake a Companion out of a Zahn trance by shouting to it," said the man contemptuously. "Even a Delta function student should know that!" He threw himself at Bond who, still shouting Solita's name, leapt over the counter to brave the steel needles, hoping they were more to frighten him than to kill him. He felt one of them stab his arm as he fell behind the counter taking the bell, invoice book and skeins of wool with him.

"Solita!" he shouted again. The light changed. The box lit up as if a little fire blazed in it.

"Bond? Is that you, Bond? Is it rescue?" asked a girl's voice. The man appeared astounded and stood as if the steel needles had pinned him into the air in some way.

"Audio defence!" commanded Bond, desperately trying to recall all he could about this Wirdegen enemy who had appeared out of nowhere and who now tried to grab him and to set a small disc against his forehead.

"Bond, is that you?" asked Solita again.

"Audio defence!" screamed Bond. "Yes, this is Bond – *Bond*. I wouldn't deceive you. Read my bio-phase! Audio defence! This is override instruction." He shouted a series of numbers, thrashing his head backwards and forwards as he cried out. The disc placed against his temple slid down, scraped the side of his face and struck his ear as he managed to knee the man in the side. The woman toppled like a heavy doll across his legs, trapping him. But even as it seemed as if he might be caught, a thin, keening sound made itself heard, rapidly rising and swooping up into the range of inaudibility.

Several things then happened at once. A fine shiver ran through the shop. There was a shocking uproar, not from the transistor but from a little dog tied to a parking meter howling dismally and tugging at its leash. Several car horns sounded in the street outside and could not be turned off, and glasses shattered on nearby tables, exploding into glittering daggers of glass. The woman on top of Bond clasped her hands over her head and tried to crawl towards the door. The bearded figure hanging over Bond suddenly collapsed. One minute it was suspended above him, powerful and menacing, the next it was collapsing with a slow, billowing grace. The pale, goatish face shining between the upper and lower nests of hair, and the live yellow eyes, vanished as if they had been sucked back into darkness. The woman did not vanish in the same way but fell to one side in an apparent faint. Bond pushed his way out from under empty clothes and, shuddering, seized the Companion and clumped out of the shop.

Once back on the pavement he grew as swift and as graceful as a bird, sliding in and out between passers-by, clasping the black box to his chest as if he was warming it back to life. No-one followed him.

4. Patchwork

Early on Friday morning, the morning on which Bond began his search for the Companion, just when Philippa found she was unable to sleep any longer and David was mumbling, "There's no way round it, I've got to get up and face the world," there was the sound of a terrible fight. The only voice to be heard was Dora's and it went on and on, punctuated with thumps like commas. Then the sound of breaking china came as if it were a full stop. A door opened and slammed. Hasty footsteps made their way down the hall.

Philippa sat up like a jack-in-a-box, her hair standing on end as if with terror. "What was that?" she said. "Oh dear, oh dear . . . " Her voice started off in its usual bright tone, but sank down into a whispery mixture of squeaks and hisses like a bicycle pump needing oil and repairs.

"Yesterday was awful, but this is worse. *Now* what's wrong?"

"Only one way to find out," said David, leaping out of bed and pulling on his dressing gown.

Jake was standing in the hall already wearing her cowboy hat even though it was only seven o'clock in the morning. Her pyjama top didn't match her pyjama pants, and the sleeves and legs were much too short for her anyway.

"I said something," she told David at once, "and it started a fight."

"What did you say?" asked her father.

"Jake, what's happened?" asked Philippa appearing in the hallway.

"You take yours and I'll take mine," said David. "Keep them clear of anything valuable and we'll see if we can't work it out. Come on Jake – into the living room!"

Jake marched ahead of him like the Lone Ranger with a gun held to his back. "The next time you get married, let's have nothing but boys," she flung at him over her shoulder. Once in the living room David sat on the new, floral settee and patted the empty space next to him. Jake looked at it suspiciously, but after a moment she moved forward and sat down stiffly beside him.

"Jacqueline – Jake," David corrected himself. "You can't be enjoying any of this very much."

"What's new!" said Jake sarcastically. Her lips barely opened enough to let the words through.

"There won't be a next time you know," said David. "You only get married for the second time once, and I'd like to have you here with me as much as I can. Please believe me, even though I may have been a neglectful father this past year."

"But she's an absolute wimp!" exclaimed Jake. "Not Philippa – she's okay. I mean the other one. I knew she would be, straight off."

"Dora," said David. "You know her name."

"Dora then!" Jake shrugged. "She's got a whole lot of love comics in a box under her bed and she's got some cream called *Gro-Bust* that she rubs on her chest at night."

David laughed despite himself, but he looked sad too. He had the sort of talented, lively face which could do both at once. "Poor old Dora!" he said. "She's a dear when you get to know her."

"She keeps on telling me how crazy you are about her mother," Jake complained, "and what a nice time you had in Australia. It really bugs me."

"Did you not want to come here?" asked David, sidestepping the issue. "I know Pet wasn't very keen. She's never wanted me to visit you out on the farm either."

Jake felt uneasy at the mention of her mother. After a pause she said, "Yes, I wanted to come. I really wanted to see you, but now you seem like someone else pretending to be you, and somebody different from the one you used to be."

"I *am* different," said David, "but you're different too. And truly, Jake – you still feel like part of me." Jake said nothing. "I'm arranging for us to have some time to spend on our own, just the two of us," he told her anxiously.

"See?" Jake cried with a sort of sad triumph. "You've got to *arrange* it, but you don't have to arrange to see *them* – Dora and Lewis, I mean."

Now it was David's turn to be silent. "It's not fair, but that's the way it is," he said at last.

Before his eyes, Jake's tense face relaxed a little and a slightly different expression began to form.

"That's right!" she agreed. "As long as no-one tries to fool me about things." She actually seemed comforted although David could not understand why.

"What was all the noise about, anyway?" he asked cautiously.

Jake's mouth curled up at the corners. "She got onto me about my hair and kept on about how good her hairdresser was, and I'd look better if it was shaped and you know – la la la!"

"What does 'la la la' mean this time?" queried David.

"It means the music going on and on, but no real tune," said Jake. "Just la la la – you know. Anyway, I said if she came to stay with me she could visit my dentist."

"Oh dear," said David wearily. "She hates those braces."

"I thought she might. She yelled and threw some books and a china thing at me – a kitten with a basket of flowers or something. She actually got me with one book – Anne of Green Gables I think it was." Jake rubbed her arm thoughtfully. "I have to admit that she was quick on the draw – and she shot to kill."

The door opened and Philippa entered, scanning the fireplace for the hearth brush and shovel. "How's yours," she asked.

"Struck by Anne of Green Gables but she'll survive," David answered. "What about yours?"

"Full of despair about her teeth and her broken china kitten. It sure gets the morning going with a swing, doesn't it? Just think – we might have been wasting all this time in bed," joked Philippa.

Lewis ambled out of the sunporch sucking his thumb. He leaned against the door and sighed gustily.

"I'll always wake up bad-tempered in that room," Jake confided to David when Philippa had gone. "It's like sleeping in strawberry cheesecake. Couldn't I sleep in the sunporch with Lewis?"

Lewis was so alarmed at the idea that he took his thumb out of his mouth. "No way!" he said vehemently. "Suppose the boys at school heard about it? I can just hear them – 'Lewie's got a girlfriend, Lewie's got a girlfriend!' No way!"

"He's very modest," explained David. "If I come into the bathroom while he's in the bath he covers himself with the facecloth!"

Lewis, looking embarrassed at the mere suggestion that he was ever naked in the bath, vanished back into the sunporch.

"Let's get breakfast for the others," suggested David. "This is a work day for me. We can carry on our conversation over the toaster."

"You can send me home if you like," Jake offered.

"I don't like!" said David angrily. "After less than a day? I'm not so feeble that I give in that quickly, and nor are you. So we've both changed! Big deal. If I'd stayed with your mother we'd still have changed. We're all metamorphic Jake, we change all the time. If we didn't, it'd be boring."

Meanwhile, Dora, largely recovered and secretly rather thrilled with the results of her dramatic fury, was helping Philippa sweep up the tragic, broken remnants of her china kitten. She picked up a piece and discovered a kitten's eye looking reproachfully at her. She almost wept again.

"I've tried!" she stated in a martyred voice. "Lord knows I've tried, Mum, but it's like sharing a room with – with King Kong! I think she's sold herself to the forces of evil."

"What nonsense, Dora! She's probably just feeling very lonely all on her own," said Philippa.

"How can she be lonely?" demanded Dora. "We're all here to be friends with!"

"Yes, but it might take a little time, dear. More than we first thought."

"But she teased me about my braces!" cried Dora. "Mum, what's wrong with wanting to look nice?"

"Nothing at all," comforted Philippa in a resigned voice. "That's why you're going to have your hair cut today, though personally I don't think it really needs it."

"Shaped!" Dora corrected her. "I'm having it shaped, not cut."

"Shaped then," said her mother. "I think you talk about hair and clothes too much sometimes."

Dora frowned. Then suddenly her face cleared and she smiled very happily. "I expect I'm insecure," she said, cheering up. "All the magazines say that the children of broken marriages are insecure."

"Who wants to be secure anyway?" Philippa asked lightly. "Life ought to be a little bit dangerous. That's what makes it exciting!"

"Jake isn't insecure," Dora went on, sounding pleased with herself. "She's too tough to be insecure."

"Poor Jake, then, I say," commented Philippa. "There – that's the lot I think." She picked up the brush and shovel.

"I wish she'd go home," declared Dora. "Everything was okay until she came Lone Rangering along."

"Dearest, you go and see *your* father – whenever we can catch him in one place long enough. Jake and David want to see each other too. She is his only child."

"I thought Lewis and I were supposed to be David's children too," argued Dora petulantly. "Don't we count now that Jake's here?"

Philippa tapped her on the crown of the head with the hearth brush. "Don't you play games with me!" she scolded Dora. "You know just what I mean."

Dora threw her arms about Philippa so forcibly that some of the china fragments shot out of the little shovel onto the floor again. Having both hands full, Philippa had to use the hearth brush to show her affection and this time patted Dora's bottom with it.

"I meant to be good," said Dora. "I meant to be a wonderful, understanding sister but she doesn't like me. And I don't like her."

"Come on, honey. It's a working day for David, remember? And I've got lots of things to get done before your appointment with Mr Chopperlox."

"I love Mr Chopperlox," said Dora in a dreamy voice. "He really understands me. He's a wonderful hairdresser."

They all sat round the table in the dining alcove. Breakfast was normally eaten off the kitchen bench or breakfast bar, but today the table was properly set and sported a small vase of flowers. This was done in an effort to help them all get over the stormy events of the morning. Dora and Jake carefully avoided looking at each other. Philippa noticed and after a while she swapped places with Dora. "It's easier not to look at Jake from here," she said.

Lewis ate with enormous care. He was usually rather a noisy eater, crunching apples and toast and drinking with appreciative slurping noises. Now he drank with dainty sips, looking warily from left to right as he did so.

"It's been a rough morning," said David, trying not to look too anxiously at the clock. "You girls – just cool it for today if you possibly can. I know, I just *know* there's a way round this but there you are – we're a very patchwork family. That may be charming in its own way, but it takes a little more effort to make it work." He paused and looked at each one of them in turn. Then he smiled. "Now. Suppose this Saturday we go to that pony-trekking place out on the peninsular – um, Rackham Rides –

and have a day just wandering over the hills together. We all know Jake's an accomplished horsewoman – her letters talk of nothing else – and the rest of us can more than get by."

Jake cast a longing glance towards her cowboy hat. She looked as if she couldn't wait to climb in under its all-concealing shadow.

"Rackham Rides!" cried Philippa. "David, that's inspired! It'd be lovely to get out of the house – go on a trek over the hills and through Webster's Valley. You'd love it Jake. It's beautiful."

Dora's mouth opened slowly. Next to books about families and ballet, she enjoyed books about horses and easily imagined herself on a wonderful palomino mare, winning the dressage and the open jumping sections at a big agricultural show. *What perfect understanding there is between this young rider and her horse,* the announcer would say, *she's getting an extra round of applause from the crowd just because they look so beautiful together.* She had always been jealous when David read excerpts from Jake's letters about galloping along the old coach road or jumping hedges and logs. Now they could ride together. But . . .

"Not Webster's Valley!" she cried in dismay. "Everyone knows it's haunted. The trees change places."

"The ghosts have never bothered us before," David said, looking surprised. "I thought you'd jump at the idea, Dora."

"I do, but not in a haunted place," Dora pleaded. "Everyone says it changes, sometimes the trees get taller overnight and paths shift around in it. Everyone knows."

"The short treks are rather too short for what I had in mind," said David. "I thought we could make a day of it – what do you think, Jake?"

Jake looked up rather desperately. "But I ride all the time at home! I get sick of horses." She used her Lone Ranger voice. "You all go. Don't worry about me. I'll be jake." She laughed a little at her pun but nobody else made a sound. There was dead silence.

"So! No-one likes my idea. We'll have to think of something else then," said David at last in a controlled, neutral voice. "Look, I have to rush. I'm late already."

Jake hunched her shoulders slightly and colour flooded her cheeks as an atmosphere of disapproval and gloom settled on them again like a grey fog, deadening the taste of marmalade and fresh orange juice. For some reason Lewis felt sorry for her. "I'll show you my collection of feathers later on," he whispered. "I've got a really beautiful one." Jake smiled at him gratefully.

Later on while Philippa washed the dishes, Jake and Dora stood side by side drying them without exchanging a single word. Once or twice Jake was on the verge of telling them that the real reason she didn't want to go horse-riding was not that she was bored with it – but that she was afraid of it. However then everyone would realize that she had told David many lies in her letters, and she did not want her courageous, adventurous image destroyed. So instead of speaking out she remained silent, and even smiled proudly though she was not feeling proud. She wore her cowboy hat and kept it pulled forward so that all anyone could see was a slightly cynical smile and not the worried blue eyes further up under the brim.

5. Escaping

Bond had no idea where he was. Once free of the shop he whirled away, uncertain of whether he was a victim or a winner. He missed the School desperately and missed the vast possibility of the Universe, too large to be merely confusing. He needed somewhere where he could sit and talk to Solita, to find out what a Companion could do for him apart from driving the enemy away. He needed time to remember all he could about the Wirdegen. Yet all the time he drifted he automatically sought out sensations, smells, contrasts of colour, textures and constructions. He matched the way things looked with the way they felt. He touched tin, wood and plastic; silk, nylon and cotton; and turned the pages of books. His clever fingers ran over the engraved surfaces and milled rims of coins as he bought fruit and bread. He studied and recorded buttons, snap fasteners, greeting cards, magazines, nails and bolts, electronic toys, flowers, bathroom fittings, cassettes, earrings, pottery, cakes and cookbooks. Everything Bond felt he recorded for the Inventory.

In the window of a video shop various television sets were tuned in to a morning programme intended for women at home. A fair-headed girl looked out of every set. Her face was repeated half a dozen times. Her mouth moved energetically as she spoke but the sound was turned off so nothing could be heard. Her eyes sparkled as she looked warmly and intimately out of each box, but no-one bothered to look back at her or to try and read her bright red lips. She could have been either blessing or cursing the world. Bond nodded to her but as he moved past something happened. The girl's image wavered then split up into seven different images, all overlapping each other and each one a different colour. For a moment she became a rainbow girl, while at the same time the music broadcast into the street went out of tune then howled as if the shop was full of resentful wolves. People looked up as he went by but not at him.

"I don't know what to do," Bond said aloud, and then found himself going past a coffee bar which had a tiny, bricked courtyard holding tables like tea-trays on spindly legs with striped umbrellas hovering protectively over them. He bought himself a long glass of orange juice and some sandwiches and sat down in a corner. Apart from one couple who were very involved with each other, he was the only person there.

"Solita," he addressed the box in a low voice, "I'm here on my first test so I'm in enforced isolation. I have no way of getting in touch with the School or warning them about the Wirdegen. Did you manage to warn them in any way?"

"Bond, I was jammed," Solita replied. "My field responses are damaged. I can't make contact with the School but if contact was broken both ways I would be inert." Her voice was calm and untroubled and for some reason this made Bond feel very lonely.

"My pulse is still alive," he said looking at his wrist. "That means the School can certainly trace us and probably detect alarm, but they won't be able to tell just what's wrong. If the Wirdegen get us, would they be able to gain access to the Inventory?"

"They could get direct access through me," Solita answered. "Remember that I am also back in the School, interfaced with several direct access points. I can be withdrawn if the School is approached however. The School could break my connections. I'm not really here. You, on the other hand, *are* here and could be held for some sort of ransom."

"What can I do? How can I warn them?" asked Bond. He stared blankly across the little tables. "The School may have to sacrifice me." He took a deep breath and managed a smile. "Well, I'm Galgonquan and I can work things out. Let me see. Catalogue and calculate! What do I know of the Wirdegen?" He closed his eyes to enable him to better recall the lessons the School had taught him. "I know they broke away from the Galgonqua millions of years ago – they're our wicked cousins with some of the same tricks that we have. I know that they're pirates of knowledge, and that they steal, then trade, technology and ideas to societies, often before those societies are capable of handling them properly."

"They appear on the surface of a planet such as this," added Solita, "in forms similar to the ones we wear but rather more uncertain. They're not as clever as we are and these forms can be torn apart by certain audio frequencies, though they reconstitute themselves in time."

"Yes, it was lucky I remembered that!" said Bond feeling pleased with himself.

"But I cannot defend you in such a way again until I have been recharged at some energy source," Solita reminded Bond. "I am seriously depleted." Bond arched his eyebrows and pulled a rueful face. "I can only warn you of an enemy presence close by," Solita continued. "There is never only one of them. Even now there could be several watching us outside my range."

"Yes – and that one with the yellow eyes will reform," added Bond. "I wish we could tell the School to relocate."

As he mumbled away to his Companion he knew that in actual fact his sister lay within the probationers' part of the School, floating out in space beyond the moon. The Companion spoke to Bond here, and back in the School the lips of Solita in a trance should move and speak too, though as things stood Bond could not be sure that this was happening. And now as never before Bond understood that talking to a sister was not just a matter of words but of tones of voice and expression, which he was missing badly. For the first time in his life he felt forlorn – there was no other word for it – and missed the company of the School and the support of the great Inventory of the Galgonqua, the catalogue of which every Galgonquan was a special part. It was frightening for Bond to be in touch with Solita in her present form. As his sister she was warm and laughing – teasing him because he was so sure of himself, so anxious to take his first test, and so certain he would do well. His thoughts had been able to interlock with hers more closely than they could with anybody else's thoughts. But sitting here, even with her voice murmuring out of the box before him, he missed the warmth of true sharing. He tried to be practical.

"It's true, isn't it, that the Wirdegen can flip themselves through space just like we do?"

"True enough," answered the Companion.

"But I'm not allowed to travel like that down here," said Bond dejectedly. "If I do flip through space I'll displace time. I'm not clever enough yet to do it perfectly."

"Neither are they!" said the Companion. "But they probably don't care."

"Then I have to leave the city," Bond decided, "stick to the original plan. If the School can follow us, it will probably be able to find us there." Unexpectedly he placed his hand on his chest. "That's funny," he exclaimed.

Solita did not reply. In this form she responded to questions or commands, she assessed situations and gave advice, but she had nothing to say in response to Bond's exclamation or to the sudden burning he felt on his skin. "My stone!" he said in wonderment. "The green stone my father gave me! It just burnt me." He frowned. "Why, I wonder? It might be a message, a trap – or it mightn't even mean anything."

Just at that moment Bond hated this small city. Every corner was a blank corner, street names made little sense and there was not a single face he could recognize and be able to say with certainty – *I know that person is a friend.* The hot twinge the stone had given him had died away and was relaced by something different. Not by something outside but a tug from inside. The stone was trying to tell him something.

"Solita –" he began but she interrupted him.

"We are being observed," she stated almost languidly. The Companions advised and calculated but they experienced no real emotion. They could not even be properly frightened. All feelings were shut up in the figure asleep in the School, connected to the machine. Everyone had a turn at working connected with the machine. In time Bond would become part of it too, for a while – if he survived.

Bond rose unhurriedly from the table, his face impassive, and moved out of the courtyard. He pretended to look in a shop window. Reflected in the glass he saw many cars which, once set free by a green light at the corner, shot by like a school of fish, but one of them – a great black shark – was trying to draw alongside him. He could only see the shapes of the people inside it, not their faces. He began to skate faster.

They go about so openly! he thought, amazed. *They could have kept their presence secret from me but they've given Solita a chance to warn me - they're frightening me and letting me run!* "There's no sense in it!" he said aloud, shaking his head as he hurried on.

The traffic lights turned red and both Bond and the car came to a standstill a few metres apart. A door opened. However Bond was able to turn to the left and take dangerous advantage of a gap to skate across the street and to leave the car behind. He found himself crossing a little, grassy square. There was no place to hide. It was like a green tablecloth crossed with the diagonal lines of two paths, pinned to the earth by a tree at each corner. Under these trees, only a few metres from the flow of traffic, mothers played with their toddlers, lovers embraced, a solitary man read a book. Even in flight Bond blinked and recorded. The wheels of his skates sounded louder as he got away from the traffic into the centre of the square. As he fled, the stone tugged at him and he veered to the right in an involuntary response to its summons.

There was a screech of tyres, a panic-stricken blast on a car horn, and a great eruption of noise. The car that had been pursuing him was keeping him in sight by driving in the wrong direction up a one-way street on one side of the square.

Bond skated frantically across the road before an approaching tide of traffic. The pursuing car, having completed half a circuit of the square, now came at him again, travelling this time with the flow of traffic and closing on him. He still could not see who was in the car, but he knew it was after him and he was desperate to keep ahead, not knowing what strange weapons or means of control they might possess. At any moment they might give up this clumsy means of pursuit for something more subtle and effective – a flip or a jump through space – but perhaps in the city even the Wirdegen feared the effect of a jump which twisted not only space but time itself.

"Evade," instructed Solita. "They are close." A slot of shadow appeared to Bond's left. He whisked into a long, narrow alley between two shops. There was a notice asking that the entrance be kept clear of vehicles at all times but a fraction of an instant later, to Bond's astonishment and horror, the big black car turned across the path of a cyclist and careered into the alleyway. Bond hadn't thought there was sufficient room for the car but it managed to fit in, just grazing the walls on either side, and he realized it was blocking his only exit. There were windows set high up but they were all shut, and in fact looked as if they had never been opened. Skating at full speed, Bond burst into a square grey courtyard filled with empty crates, cardboard boxes and a lot of rubbish bins. Several back doors of shops opened into this yard. The car was right on his heels. It could have run him down if it had wanted to.

"Can you lift me?" he shouted.

"Evade!" commanded Solita, the pitch of her voice blurring a little, sounding more machine-like than it had before. A door opened and Bond saw a hand throwing paper into the courtyard, most of which missed the big rubbish bins. He seized the edge of the door, jerked it wide open and spun his way in, pushing a surprised young woman to one side. He banged the door behind him, automatically checking it for bolts and slamming the only one home.

"Hey! What are you doing?" screamed the girl. He had burst into a workshop filled with machines, two printing presses, a paper guillotine and racks of paper and card of different colours and sizes. Bond shot in between the printing presses without hesitation, evading one man and causing another to drop the pile of blank, pink paper he was carrying. Bond banged his hip on a protruding piece of machinery and then was gone almost before they realized he was among them. Behind him he heard a splintering crash. The bolt burst off the door with the impact of something driving against it from the outside. Indignant cries rose again at this second and more violent invasion. Bond slid between two offices and into a shop filled with paper, pens, paints and envelopes and saw his way clear before him. He rushed headlong through the shop and out the glass doors onto the footpath, where he spun around looking for a new direction.

Once more he vaguely sensed the stone nudging him in some way. Raising his eyes Bond saw a large, glittering sign that seemed to draw him towards it – MR CHOPPERLOX, UNISEX HAIR STYLIST, it read. Parked beneath the sign was a battered, green car and leaning across from the passenger's side, staring at him as if she had been waiting for him for a long time, was a girl with blonde, bubbly curls. Their eyes met. She reached over behind her and opened the back door of the car. Bond raced across the road, his hands clasped over his head as if he expected something to fall from out of the sky. Narrowly avoiding a motorcycle he reached the car, threw himself in and heard the door slam behind him.

"Object anomaly," said Solita in his ear, and Bond felt the cold, shivery feeling that generally meant he was losing control of a temporary shape. *I'm going to change back!* he thought with terror, lying as flat as he could.

"There they go," said the girl dropping back into the front seat. "I don't think they saw you." Bond's stone burnt him with its own cold fire and, peering despairingly through the gap between the two front seats, he saw the reflection in the rear vision mirror of the girl who had rescued him. She was pretending to pat her hair into place.

"Here comes my mother," she hissed. "Lie flat!" As she threw a rug over him Bond noticed that on a chain about her neck she wore a stone, larger than his own, but at heart the same stone as the one he wore, which at that very moment melted away like an ice crystal under his palm. The shivery feeling stopped. His stone had found itself, but at least for the present he was going to be able to maintain the heroic shape he had invented back in his School.

6. Rescuing

Jake sat in a cane chair in Lewis's room while he showed her his treasured collection of bird feathers. "This is the most beautiful one," he was saying as he held up a very soft, white feather. It was so fine it moved gently with the breath of his words. He laid it down and took up another from the long box. "I found this one up in the hills. I think it's from an eagle." Lewis dreamed of eagles sometimes, and the mere words 'golden eagle' made him feel as if he might grow wings himself and become a flying boy. Once he had started to write a book called 'A Pair of Eagles' and he had written three and a half pages before he lost his pencil box for a week. By the time he found the box again the inspiration had gone.

"There aren't any eagles in New Zealand," said Jake, so regretfully that Lewis forgave her for reminding him.

"An eagle could get blown over from Australia," he suggested hopefully, stroking his feather with love. "That's how waxeyes got here — blown over from Australia. It happens all the time." Immediately he said it, he thought it must be true. He could just see the eagle, buffeted by strong winds, being carried along in a cloud of little, green, fluttering birds – the waxeyes – its wings spread majestically, its fierce yellow eyes staring down through the writhing layers of angry, turbulent air.

Beside him Jake was thinking of herself as a fierce eagle blown out of its native surroundings into a new world where there was a gentle, kindly, easy life full of pretty things, encouraging her to be gentle and pretty too. She was completely certain, however, that she must not begin thinking that she had any part in such a life because it really belonged to someone else, and once she came to think it might be hers in any way it would be taken away from her. She knew this in the same way she knew she must not let people carry heavy things for her because by now she had learned to carry them for herself, and it was not a thing that any sensible person would want to learn twice over.

The door opened. "Hi," said Dora brightly. Jake and Lewis turned, both surprised by her happy voice, and saw at once that her voice was probably the only happy part of her. Her curls were a little shorter and a little neater than they had been this morning and she smelt of hairdressing potions, but her eyes were wide and anxious as if she had just caught a glimpse of a possible werewolf or vampire. She smiled weakly at Jake.

"Hi," replied Jake.

"What are you doing?" asked Dora in a chatty voice.

"Talking about eagles," answered Lewis.

Dora suddenly decided to tell them what was troubling her. She knelt down beside Lewis, but it was Jake she looked at – her expression asking for her help and at the same time defying her to do her worst. "Can you keep a deadly secret?" she asked, twisting the greenstone at her throat. "I wouldn't bring you into it, but I don't know what to do. I've done something absolutely awful!"

"What is it?" asked Jake, beginning to look interested.

"I saved a boy from gangsters," said Dora. "He was being chased and I just opened the back door of the car and let him in – not actually *on* the back seat that is, but down in between the front seats and the back one. I covered him up with the car rug, and Mum came and got in and drove us home."

"Where is he now then?" asked Lewis, astounded.

"Locked in the garage," said Dora, and she began to cry. Lewis took no notice of the tears – Dora crying was nothing unusual – but Jake stared in surprise.

"What are you crying for?" she asked incredulously but without malice.

"He's locked in our garage!" exclaimed Dora, as if this explained everything. "If David and Mum find out, they'll kill me."

"Don't be silly! They wouldn't kill a snail, not even if they found it in amongst the cabbages!" Jake replied.

"But they'll be mad," said Dora. "I'm not even allowed any pets!"

"They said we can get a kitten sometime soon," said Lewis eagerly.

"Hang on! It's not the same!" declared Jake. "We're talking about a person, not a pet. They'd help a person who was being chased by gangsters."

"Mum wouldn't believe they were gangsters," Dora muttered.

"Do *you* believe they were gangsters?" Jake asked. "I mean to say – gangsters? It's pretty hard to believe."

"He came running out of a shop," said Dora. In her mind's eye the scene was as fresh as if it was taking place before her all over again. She had been gazing at the myriad of reflections on the glass shop window when suddenly, surfacing from that reflecting world as if swimming up through deep water, she had seen a golden boy, fleeing from unseen enemies.

"He came skating out of a shop," she corrected herself, recalling the way he had spun through the door in a blur of colour, his pale hair shining in the afternoon light.

"He might've been shop-lifting," suggested Jake. She had a way of half looking down at the floor and smiling, then looking up under her eyebrows that Dora found unnerving.

"It wasn't a shop-lifting sort of shop," said Dora crossly. "It just sold cards and envelopes and wedding invitations –"

"I still don't know how you can be sure he's a goodie," stated Jake. "Suppose it was the Mafia after him. They might have got blown over from

Australia like waxeyes, or it might have been some legal organization like the SIS or the CIA who're after him – or his father, or something."

"The CIA's in America!" cried Dora.

"They get everywhere. They're probably checking us out all the time – that's what Manley says." Jake stopped abruptly. She had not wanted to mention Manley.

"Who's Manley?" asked Dora, confused to find a stranger suddenly brought in to the conversation.

"He's my mother's friend," mumbled Jake. Her lips barely moved as she spoke.

"You'd make a really neat ventriloquist!" commented Lewis respectfully.

Dora looked at Jake with renewed interest lighting her eyes. "Is he a close friend?" she asked delicately. If Jake's mother married again there mightn't be the need for any more awkward visits like these.

"He's a pain in the neck," spat Jake vehemently. "Forget him. What about this rescued boy of yours, Dora? Did he tell you anything?"

"No – didn't have a chance. Mum arrived almost at once and now he's locked in the garage."

"He might run out of oxygen," said Lewis, staring at Jake and trying to talk without moving his lips.

"There's plenty of oxygen in the garage. It gets in under the door," Jake said knowledgeably. "We ought to check him out though. Do you have to pinch the keys?"

"No, just get them from the kitchen," said Lewis, "and lock up afterwards so no-one pinches our lawn mower and things."

Philippa was surprised when they came in to get the key, and even more surprised when the three of them walked out of the house together and across to the garage. She watched them roll up the door. Last night after the children had gone to bed she and David had had – not a quarrel so much as a disagreement, and she had felt very insecure all day. The new house and the new things in it, the tree-lined street and the nice neighbourhood suddenly felt fragile, like a cleverly-painted screen she had put up around her to hide the real, fierce world beyond. She was also frightened that there would be other disagreements that would turn into real quarrels and that once again she would find she had married someone she did not really want to live with. Thoughts such as these passed like dark spirits through her head and she felt as though the sparkling kitchen was not really hers – that nothing in the house had any history or permanence, everything was too new and she felt that she had no real place of her own.

Once inside the garage Dora unlocked the car and said, "Are you there?" wondering as she did so if she had perhaps imagined the whole thing, and then, *Suppose he's smothered under that rug?* She had an uneasy feeling that he might not be there at all. However Bond rose up from under the rug looking like an amazing clown, his pale face smiling and faintly luminous in the shadows of the garage. Lewis and Jake clambered into the front of the car and Dora got in the back with Bond. All four stared at each other like conspirators who weren't altogether sure just what they were conspiring about.

"Thank you," Bond was saying. "I think I must have lost them by now. I must be out of their range. There's the whole city to look through."

Something about the words he used made Jake regard him very closely and she suddenly felt a sensation like pins and needles all over her body but could not explain why. Taken piece by piece Bond was ordinary enough.

There was nothing impossible in his many pockets or his white hair or his wonderful transistor radio connected by a silver wire to his ear, or even in the way his hand lay on his chest as if he was hiding a bullet hole. Yet Jake felt as if Dora had rubbed a lamp and a genie had appeared.

"Who were they?" Dora asked Bond. "They weren't the CIA were they?"

Bond looked at her with a hesitation in his expression as if he was having to wait for her question to be absorbed into his mind. He did not reply immediately.

"Oh no," he said at last. "It was nothing like that. It was — er, a family matter."

"Was it your father?" asked Jake.

"Relations," replied Bond cautiously. "Distant relations. How far did we travel to get here?"

"Oh, a long, long way!" said Dora reassuringly.

Jake saw at once that this strange boy believed exactly what Dora said, although *she* knew very well that Dora simply meant that they had driven out of town – three kilometres at the very most. And, perhaps because the circumstances were so peculiar already, she noticed something else that also seemed strange to her. Bond looked at the three of them with an expression that reminded her of her father, though he didn't look at all like David. It was the expression of responsibility, of deciding to do something he did not want to do for the sake of others' happiness.

"Thank you for opening the door. I'm very grateful. But I mustn't stay. I have to move on."

Dora, who had been horrified at the thought of Bond staying in the back of the car, was now horrified at the thought of his going away. He stood for something too new and exciting to be lost. "Oh no!" she cried. "We can hide you here."

"How can we?" stated Jake reasonably. "You need room to hide someone, enough room to be warm in and to have something to eat. There's not even a bush in this place that you could hide behind. Nothing tangled."

Dora thought Jake was criticizing the new house, finding it plain and bare after her own country estate with its huge garden and woodland and stables. "I suppose you have masses of bush where you live," she said resentfully.

Jake frowned, then her mouth turned up at the corners very slowly as if a smile, amused and not at all sinister, was trying hard to be born. "We could hide him and ten more like him where I live," she said. "Come on, Dora, be fair! It's too well-kept here to hide anyone for long." It was the first time she had called Dora by name.

"I should leave now," repeated Bond, "but I need to sleep first if I can. Could I sleep in the car for an hour or two? I'd be most grateful."

"You'd better keep down then," said Jake, "because my Dad's car is just turning in at the gate."

"Lie down where you were before," hissed Dora. "I'll cover you up again and we'll come back later on. Don't let David see you." It occurred to Dora that she didn't even know this boy's name. She could only call him 'you'.

"Don't look so guilty," Jake warned her. "Just stay cool!"

However feeling guilty was part of Dora's way of enjoying the excitement. It was as if she was acting all the time for an invisible audience inside her head. *Hooray for Dora, the brave and beautiful!* they shouted whenever she came onto the stage. The gestures she made for their benefit were easily seen by anyone, but the applause was heard only by Dora herself.

David's car glided quietly into the garage. "Hello kids! It's nice of you to come and meet me. It makes me feel wanted." He spoke to them all but it was Jake on whom his gaze rested.

"We were just getting something out of the car," Dora said, so casually that Jake thought

David would have to be suspicious. He didn't seem to notice.

"I hope it wasn't the steering wheel," he joked. It wasn't very funny but Lewis laughed so hard he nearly choked. "The steering wheel!" he repeated to himself and laughed again.

"I'll carry your briefcase," offered Dora.

"Really? That's very civil of you, Dora." As they walked up to the house, Lewis and David in front and the two girls trailing behind, Philippa appeared on the steps to meet them.

"She's put on a different dress and some lipstick! That shows they're in love," Dora murmured to Jake, her voice dreamy and sentimental.

"She'll soon get sick of it," said Jake cynically. "Not love - but getting changed when she doesn't have to."

"I like getting dressed up for things," countered Dora defiantly.

"You would!" grumbled Jake, but she had a lot on her mind and didn't sound as contemptuous as she would have done earlier in the day.

7. Plans and Disguises

The patchwork family sat down to dinner rather self-consciously, smiling politely at one another.

"No more fights," announced Philippa, "because not only have I cooked this delicious meal, but I've been working out how to turn a corner of the living room into a bedroom for Jake. It would be like a sort of bedsitter for the duration of the holidays. I know someone we could borrow a folding bed from, and we could fit that in behind the sofa —" she turned to Jake, "if you don't mind having a leftover bit of space, that is, Jake?"

"I don't need much," Jake mumbled, turning red. "I don't want to be any trouble."

"Dora's room is so full of Dora's things," continued Philippa. "We thought it might work out to put you two together, but now I can see you're two totally different propositions."

"From your photo you looked more like Dora's kind – not like a tough cowboy," added Lewis, and wondered why his mother frowned at him and said "Lewis!" in her 'scolding' voice.

"People's things do make a difference," David agreed. "I like people, but sometimes I think it would be nice to get to a beginning place where there were just the people themselves – none of their things. No cowboy hats or 'op' shop jerseys . . . "

"No red car," said Jake sternly. David looked at her for a second, then nodded rather ruefully. "All right – no red car. No green car. Just people themselves. No other clues."

"No *clothes?*" asked Lewis, seizing his table napkin as if he might need it to cover himself at any moment.

"No hair dye . . . " added Dora generously.

" . . . or felt pens . . . " said Lewis, suddenly catching on. His felt pens were his favourite items. Drawing with his felt pens he could become anything he drew, even an eagle.

" . . . or history," said Philippa.

"No history!" agreed David, reaching for the salt. "History's the great clutterer. The world's full of people, all of us dragging our histories behind us like – like . . . "

"Like long, tangly tails," filled in Lewis quickly.

" . . . like long, tangly tails," repeated David. "It'd be nice to get to some clear place before things and history began and we could see one another very clearly and talk together like friends straight away, with no worry about the past or anyone's hair style, or what anybody wears and so on." He sighed. "Unfortunately, that can never be. Oh well, dreams are free!"

"I think a space behind the sofa would be really good," said Jake, returning to the original conversation. She was grateful to Philippa for her consideration and showed it by smiling in a way that made Dora realize that Jake could still look like her photograph if she wanted to.

"That's settled then. So – let's go for a drive after dinner, shall we?" suggested David. "We'll drive over the hills, maybe watch the moon rise over the harbour, then stop at that place that stays open late for a milk shake before heading home. What do you think?"

Dora looked dismayed. "I can't come!" she blurted out.

"Dora, I thought you of all people would back me up." David looked surprised.

"Well, we're playing a sort of game we've got to finish," she rushed on. "It's a game of Monopoly and I've got a hotel on Mayfair. We have to finish it. Besides, it would be nice for you and Mum to have some time on your own." She smiled brightly at her own ingeniousness.

Overdoing it! thought Jake. *What a fool! They must know there's no game of Monopoly set up anywhere in the house. It takes up half a room when you're playing it!*

David looked hopeful, Philippa suspicious. "Dora – you aren't up to any mischief are you? No stray cats? No plans to dye your hair?"

"Oh no!" Dora cried with great sincerity. "Truly I'm not. It's just this game we're playing – we don't want to interrupt it, do we, you kids?"

"No!" chorused Lewis and Jake obediently, with Jake wondering why she found it so hard to lie to David when it seemed that Dora found it so casy. But Dora didn't regard it as lying, merely preventing the truth from causing too much trouble.

"Well," said David. "I must admit I'd like to show Philippa the moon. She hasn't seen it before, you know."

"Yes she has," said Lewis, confused. "She's seen it lots of times."

"But the one they had last year had been put too close to the sun and was covered in blisters," said Philippa.

"Those were craters!" cried Lewis, roaring with laughter at his mother's ignorance.

"Oh Phil, darling. Let me take you away from all this. We'll test the moon – colour, texture, taste..."

"Mmm, this moon is simply delicious!" Philippa said.

"Cooked to perfection," agreed David.

"You can tell they're in love," said Dora later as they watched David and Philippa leave. "They're even holding hands walking to the garage!"

"That's a bit stupid!" commented Jake, scornfully. "It takes two hands to open the garage door!" But as they watched, it was opened using David's right hand and Philippa's left.

"Did David and your mother ever hold hands?" asked Dora. "Mum never held hands with my real father. At least not when I was looking." She wanted to think that David had never truly loved anyone until he met Philippa. Somehow that would make her as much his true daughter as Jake was.

Jake gave her a slight smile. "If Dad ever held my mother's hand it would be to make sure she didn't hit him!"

"Did she *hit* him?" cried Dora, both shocked and thrilled at what poor David must have suffered before he became a part of their family.

"I was only joking!" Jake explained. "Well — half true, half joke."

"A Jake-joke!" Lewis seemed pleased with his quick wit.

Jake ignored him. "Suppose they take your mother's car, though?" she said anxiously.

"They won't! It rattles," answereed Dora smugly. "Besides, I don't think there's much petrol in it."

Sure enough, the car that eventually backed out of the garage was David's car, although Philippa was driving, enjoying the thought of being seen in a sporty car, quieter and faster than her own. The electric window slid smoothly down. "Can you please put the milk bottles out?" called Philippa. "Don't forget or we'll have no milk for breakfast. See you later!"

Cheerfully, the three children waved them on their way.

"Now, let's get that boy out!" said Lewis with satisfaction.

"Yeah, and ask him his name this time," added Jake.

Bond told them his name. Somehow he looked even more odd sitting on the flowery sofa in their living room.

"*James* Bond! Double 0 seven! Licensed to kill?" Jake asked, smiling.

Bond turned his eyes towards her and for the first time she looked deep into them. They were blue-grey, the colour of the sea on a cloudy day, and showed no understanding at all of what she had just said. As she watched she was amazed to see comprehension flood into them as if the knowledge was suddenly supplied from thin air.

"Don't you ever stop listening to your radio?" she asked impatiently, while Dora made fluttering gestures at her in an effort to gain attention.

"Sorry!" said Bond, disconnecting the silver wire from his ear.

"I've had a terrific idea!" Dora announced. Her terrific idea was that they should disguise Bond. "White Fire won't be any good for you," she pondered. "It's got to be Midnight Appointment or Kiss of Fire."

"Kiss of fire?" queried Bond. He looked into space as he asked the question, rather than at Dora.

"I know – it's hair dye!" exclaimed Lewis before Dora could explain. "She's got a drawer full of it. What about Ginger Crunch?" he asked in an affected voice.

Dora turned red with anger. "You shouldn't go looking in my drawers reading private hair

colouring!" she declared crossly. "I don't go looking at your stupid feathers!" She turned to the
other two. "I just thought we could dye Bond's hair
as a sort of disguise."

Jake waited to see what Bond might have to say
about this but he seemed more curious than worried. Dora went to her room and fetched the bottle.
She handed it to Bond who studied the label. "The
single-step process to new, true hair colouring. It's
as easy as one, two, three." He shook the bottle,
removed the cap and smelt the lotion inside. "They
don't actually recognize me by my hair," he said
but was too curious about having his hair dyed to
turn down Dora's offer.

"Well, I think I'll be in charge of refreshments,"
said Jake. "This isn't my scene." For all that she
kept on going to the bathroom to watch from the
door while Dora fussed over Bond, finding him
such a passive patient that she went even further
and put his hair in rollers. Jake put together a tray
of crackers, cheese and fruit, thinking to herself
that a house where you could raid the fridge and
cupboards wasn't half bad. She was beginning to
feel at home here.

By the time she had finished pouring some cold
drinks, Bond was sitting with a sort of puffed-out
tea cosy on his head which was connected by a
wide, plastic tube to a machine with a windy voice.
His hair was being dried and Jake thought he
looked like a spaceman. He did not seem in the
least perturbed about being seen under a hair-dryer
but she deduced that that was probably because he

was a bit strange anyway – he even wore unusual red and black tattoos on either side of his neck. Lewis felt humiliated for him. As Jake pushed the crackers towards him, not very graciously, Bond smiled his bright smile at her.

"You're all being very good to me," he said. "You don't know anything about me."

"We go by the look!" said Dora. "You look as if you're on the right side."

"You shouldn't do that," warned Bond. "The look can be changed. I mean, you're changing the way I look now, aren't you? And some people can take off one look and put on another as easily as you might change a coat." As he said this he unbuttoned his shirt with many pockets, took it off and put it on again inside out. It was dark blue, quite plain, and changed him remarkably. "See?" he said.

Jake had eyed him with considerable doubt before. Now her eyes narrowed and something different began to show in her face. It was a distant cousin of fear – suspicion. Bond had changed his look not merely by changing his shirt. Jake imagined he had somehow managed to pull his face into a different shape, and it made the hair prickle on her head. Dora's hair did not prickle at all. Perhaps it was because Jake's hair was so very short and unshaped by the wonderful Mr Chopperlox.

"You've *got* to go by the look!" Dora remarked, surprised that there should be any doubt. "That's what it's there for, so that people can go by it. You can't wait to find out if someone's nice before you rescue them!"

"Well – *you* tell us if you're nice or not," Jake said to Bond, a challenging look on her face. Some questions need to be asked even when there is no possible answer. Jake thought her question could not be answered. However Bond tried to answer it as honestly as he could.

"I think I am good," he said. "I won't steal from you or hurt you. But I might bring trouble down on you. I'm being followed by a kind of danger – and I'll have to move on as soon as I can."

As he spoke, Dora decided Bond's hair was dry enough. She removed the dryer and the rollers so that his head was covered with glossy sausages. Then she brushed the sausages into fluffy curls. The curls, bright red and shining, made fiery ripples around his ears. "You took the colour exactly!" Dora cried with a dramatic gesture. She pulled Bond to his feet and spun him around to look at his reflection in the mirror over the mantelpiece.

"Amazing!" said Bond. "It might even – no, probably not. I'll have to go."

"Go!" wailed Dora. "But we've only disguised you! We haven't rescued you yet! Stay the night."

"Where would he sleep?" asked Lewis.

"I can't stay in your house," Bond objected, and for the first time since they had met him he looked frightened. "Believe me – I'll be all right. But I must go."

Dora ignored his protestation. "He could sleep under my bed," she suggested.

Jake saw that this might be possible. "We could smuggle him out in the morning," she said, nodding in agreement. "No big deal!"

But Bond was not convinced. "I dream!" he cried rather desperately. " I have nightmares. I talk in my sleep and describe a thousand terrible deaths, all mine."

Dora rolled her eyes skywards. There was no getting away from horror stories, she thought. But Jake, who had stood up in order to go and get some more crackers, sat down again. She leaned her elbows on her knees and propped her head in her hands. "This isn't just ordinary," she said, staring directly at Bond. "This is something weird, isn't it?"

"I have to say yes," replied Bond, "but I'm not allowed to tell. I've made serious promises of silence. I'm grateful for all you've done, but I must go now – quickly, and I'll never be heard of again and your lives won't be altered in the slightest. Whereas if you try and look after me you may suffer for it. I'm trying to be honest with you," he added, gingerly touching his newly-dyed hair as if the fiery red might actually burn him. "But I am not allowed to tell you my story. You know I am trying to escape from someone, and I'm not sure when I'll receive the help I should get. I must keep ahead for another day, and even if I can't keep ahead I must be silent."

"Keep ahead of what?" asked Dora. "Enemies?"

"Hide, and let them run past you," advised Jake.

"They won't run past," Bond said. "If I find a lonely place my friends can come and help me. They can't come to the city. Look." From one of his many pockets he extracted a map. It was folded over but still looked brand new. Bond unfolded it and spread it out over his pocketed knees. "I have to get there, for example – or there – or there."

"That's the peninsular!" exclaimed Dora peering over his shoulder. "Oh my goodness!" she said dramatically. "Brilliant!"

"What?" asked Jake. "What's so exciting?"

"We could go on the trek! Look, he's got his finger quite close to Webster's Valley."

Jake looked at the map. "Is that the place you said was haunted?" Dora closed her eyes. "Where did you get this map?" Jake asked Bond, staring more closely. "It looks – I don't know – if you look at it closely it gets sort of three-dimensional."

"Never mind where he got it," said Dora. "Bond, if you stay we can probably get you there tomorrow. Our parents will do anything for us. Anything! They want us to have a good time and to get to like each other." Dora was already involved in preparing herself to brave the ghosts, and to talk David and Philippa into going on the trek after all.

"It's no use saying we won't be altered," Jake burst out, "we're altered by it already. And suppose we did let you just walk off into the dark when there are enemies hiding in wait for you - we'd be altered by that, too!"

"How?" asked Bond.

"We'd know we were cowardly," said Jake, "and we'd always wonder what happened to you. We can't just give in."

It was Dora's turn to be impressed. "That's right! Well done, Jake!"

"You should be careful," said Bond seriously. "I might be warning you only to *appear* honest – to get sympathy I might use one small truth to eclipse another bigger one. The moon eclipses the sun."

Jake's mouth dropped open as if he had sprouted wings or turned to gold before her eyes. She sent a quick glance in Dora's direction, half looking for support. "How old are you?" she said at last, in a cautious voice. Bond said nothing. "Okay! Well, suppose we put you back out in the green car? Would you be safe there?" She spoke almost as if she had suddenly lost interest in the whole affair.

Dora was looking about, confused by Bond's answers and Jake's reactions, when she saw the milk bottles sitting in their carrier on the table. She glanced anxiously at the clock and saw that there was still time before the milkman arrived. "Lewie, run out with the milk bottles, will you please? Mum told us not to forget."

"Why don't you?" asked Lewis, but he knew that it was a foregone conclusion since he was the youngest, and that if he went quickly he would not miss much. He picked up the milk crate and ran out the door into the dark.

8. Lewis Surprised

Lewis had always enjoyed putting the milk bottles out. The tokens reminded him of game counters, and he secretly felt that if he put them out in the right way, one day he might win a prize. Sometimes he hopped out to the milk box, sometimes he jumped two steps and skipped one.

Tonight however, not wanting to miss anything, he scuttled out to the box as quickly as he could, but as he put the bottles into it something touched his shoulder. Lewis let out a squeak, so high and shrill it was almost like a whistle. As he spun around fearfully, he saw for a brief second a figure standing so close behind him he could have felt its breath if it was a breathing thing. He glimpsed a knobbly forehead and white hair. Then something cold and round like a frozen coin was placed on his forehead. He felt the circle of burning cold begin to bite into him – and then suddenly it was gone.

Lewis sighed with relief. He felt initially as if he had been changed into another shape by his fright, and then that something had entered him – not a moth or a beetle but something that burned his eyes for a moment without really hurting him. He wondered if his eyes had gone red in the dark, and as he wondered this he felt the strangest sensation inside his head. His own thoughts were being softly but remorselessly nudged aside. *Make way for me!* something was saying. *Give ME a place. Let me share your eyes, let me listen with your ears.* Lewis felt it turn around and around like a cat before it settles down and then, just as pain follows a few seconds behind a numbing blow, he felt real fear. It was like nothing he had ever felt before though he had often been frightened. This real fear was so great it seemed as if everything he was composed of — his legs, his heart, his lungs, his stomach quietly digesting crackers and cheese — had all stopped working at once. He couldn't tell whether his feet were touching the ground or not. Everything was paralysed with the electricity of terror.

Yet as quickly as this fear ate him up, it was gone. It had seemed endless, though actually within a second or two it had vanished. Whatever it was that had entered Lewis's head was a fear-eater and it ate up all the fear his mind could produce. But fear is a warning, and as the fear vanished, the warning vanished too. Lewis raced back inside and found Jake and Bond still arguing.

"I saw one!" Lewis cried. "I saw one!"

"Saw what?" asked Dora, then as realization struck her, "You can't have," she said. "How do you know?"

Lewis now stood still, looking bewildered. "I just *do* know," he stated at last. "They must have meant me to know."

This made no sense to Dora but Bond frowned.

He looked desperate. "They don't do things by mistake – not things like that," he said. "What are they trying to do? Are they trying to herd me?" He paused and looked at his Companion. "They may think I'm still defended."

"And so you are," Dora said bravely, "because you can be locked in the garage or sleep under my bed." Her voice wavered nervously as she spoke but no-one else noticed.

"Lewis might have made a mistake out there in the dark," said Jake. "It might have been someone just walking by."

Bond looked up at the electric light overhead. "There's a light like that out in the – in the –" He looked longingly at his transistor box. "Out there! There's a light, is there?"

"In the garage? Yes," said Dora.

"Then I could stay there in safety for a little while," replied Bond.

"But you can't leave the light on," Dora said. "Mum and David would see it." She thought Bond's enemies might be frightened of the light, like vampires.

"I won't need light," Bond promised her.

"Could they get into a locked car?" asked Jake. "Even if they didn't have the key?" Bond did not answer her.

Later, after taking Bond out to hide him again in the back of Philippa's car, already sustained with tea and cake and accompanied by more cake and apples in case he got hungry in the night, the three children did not return inside the house immediately. Instead they turned on the outside light and played a game of hide-and-seek in the garden. They were merely using the game as a sort of disguised guard duty but in a way it was both exciting and frightening, for the darkness that insistently lurked around corners of their garden in spite of the outside light, was alive with many chances, and beyond that again, where it got really black, the night seemed rippling with terrible possibilities. Who knew what yellow, goat-like eyes might be watching them from under smooth, yellow lids? A hand could appear from nowhere and whisk away either the hider or the seeker as a hostage to mystery.

"I've got to look after Lewis!" Dora said, and would not let him leave her side. No-one was fooled. She was almost faint with fear when it was her turn to hide. Even Lewis was no comfort, turning large eyes towards her slowly and gravely as if he was about to announce that he was not quite what he seemed. Dora would not give in to her fear however, which earned Jake's grudging respect. Nevertheless all three were relieved when after fifteen minutes of the game the driveway was lit up, the air purred, and David and Philippa drove in, full of apologies for having been longer than they had intended. Feeling rather guilty about this they felt quite unable to growl at their children for playing outside so late at night. The red car was put away beside its silent green companion, the garage was locked, and everyone went indoors.

"Let's have some supper!" suggested Philippa. "Toast and scraps. There's a little bit of strawberry jam in the bottom of the jar, and there's some left over ham and all sorts of bits and pieces. Family supper! Oh – I see you've already had some."

"We were trying to make Jake feel at home," answered Dora virtuously. Lewis just studied the floor, silently and gravely.

"We've been making plans," Dora continued, throwing Jake a look of great significance. "You know how we thought we wouldn't be able to go on the pony trek – well, we've changed our minds . . . "

Both David and Philippa looked up sharply at this announcement, and stared at the children with considerable suspicion. *No wonder,* thought Jake, *Dora overdoes everything!*

" . . . and we'd like to take a friend of Jake's, too." Dora carried on as though she was totally unaware of the suspicious looks she was being given. "He used to live near Jake but he shifted to the city last term – to *this* city, I mean. We rang him up and sort of asked him. I thought it would be okay." Philippa opened her mouth to speak, but Dora rushed in anxiously, "We're supposed to be making Jake happy. You said we had to."

David had picked up the evening paper. Now he put it down again. He had startlingly blue eyes, exactly the same colour and shape as his daughter's. "I'm being manipulated," he moaned. "I just know it. It hasn't happened for a while, but I remember the feeling distinctly. We've all suddenly turned into one big, happy family, have we?"

"Isn't that what you wanted? You should be pleased!"

"I'm delighted – but I would like to know which magic spell you used to achieve this so suddenly. And who is this friend? Will he pay for himself, or do I have to pay for him? And how is it that Jake hasn't mentioned him till now? These are deep waters, Dora."

"I only just remembered that it was this city that he moved to," mumbled Jake. "It's okay though. He's a nice guy."

"It was like doing a jigsaw puzzle," added Lewis, cryptically. "You try something in lots of different places and suddenly it fits in."

"Like Jake has suddenly fitted in – and like the trek has suddenly fitted in too?" asked David.

"You said you wanted to go on it. It was your idea, David," pleaded Dora. "You did say we could."

Philippa glanced at the three anxious faces. "Well," she said. "I don't see why not. It's a bit late to ring Rackham Rides but I'm a good enough friend to get away with it. Mind you, they're probably booked up."

She went out to the telephone. Jake saw Dora cross her fingers and reflected, with a sinking heart, that except for one thing that no-one else knew about, the trek was a very good idea. However because Dora had already proved capable of conquering the dark which frightened her, Jake knew that she had to go along with the idea and do her best. She wondered what would happen if they left Bond out by Webster's Valley and conversely, what would happen if they had to bring him back home again. He couldn't carry on living in the garage. Suddenly life seemed very complicated, as if they were all running with no place to run to. Still, they would do what they could. She believed Bond was almost telling the truth, and was confident that sooner or later they would find out what it was that he was holding back.

9. Bond Unbound

Out in the garage, Bond waited patiently until the reflections on the car windows showed he was alone. He cautiously sat up and let himself out of the car. He did not turn the light on but simply stood quietly in the dark, the Companion hanging at his side.

Bond began to glimmer slightly and then to glow in the dark. He became the core of a dim blue shine that painted other objects with a blue hue. The green car appeared a bright turquoise colour, the red one looked purple and the aluminium extension ladder shone with the colour of a low gas flame as if it was the source of the light rather than a reflection of it. The same soft light illuminated the squat shapes of paint tins, David's tools hung on a pegboard, and the blades of the push-mower, complicated with their own shadows. Bond stepped lightly onto the bumper of the green car then scrambled up to stand on the bonnet. He unscrewed the light bulb and placed it carefully on a shelf within easy reach. Then he drew a long, shiny wire from a compartment in his Companion, and inserted this into an attachment that he took from one of his many pockets. Another pocket yielded a minute screwdriver and within a short space of time he had connected the Companion to the socket of the electric light above him. He attached the ear piece once again, then scrambled down and turned the light switch on. A dry hum filled the air.

"Solita," he said.

"I'm glad you are back," Solita replied. "With no ear, there is no voice and it is a terrible thing to be mute."

"I'm sorry Solita, but I had to disconnect you to avoid suspicion. You heard what's going on though, didn't you? We're under seige but my friends are trying to get us to a place where we can keep moving. Can you recharge here?" Bond asked.

"There is more than enough energy here," answered Solita. The wind snuffled at the bottom of the garage door. "I detect Wirdegen presence," murmured Solita. "You need to sleep, Bond, or you will go into involuntary metamorphosis. You must sleep. Yes, a little sleep, a little slumber, a little folding of the hands to rest. Set me to audio defence."

"I was going to, anyway," commented Bond.

"Remember that I will not be able to maintain your appearance when in the audio defence mode," Solita cautioned him.

"That's why I wouldn't stay with the others inside," replied Bond. "I didn't want to frighten them."

He pondered about how strange it was that here, in the past – his past which was now also the present – on the planet that had been the first home of the Galgonqua, Jake and Dora seemed like his true sisters, and his real sister Solita had become just a machine and a voice. And yet she understood him as the others never could. His train of thought was interrupted as the garage door quivered as if something was searching it for a weak point through which to penetrate.

"They may break through," Bond observed unemotionally. "But you're right – I must sleep."

"I will maintain. I will lay down a spinfield until the day breaks and the shadows flee," reassured Solita in soft, even tones.

Bond did not reply. Unreeling the wire to give himself enough to reach the car he climbed into the back seat taking his luminous shadow with him rather like a child taking a teddybear to bed. He stretched out on his back as best he could with his hands folded on his chest and fell asleep immediately, as if he willed it to happen. As he slept he began to change, taking on a different shape from the one he wore in the human world. His bones seemed to shorten so that he actually fitted comfortably on the seat. His newly-dyed red hair straightened, grew longer and became streaked with blue. The shape of his hands began to reform, each becoming a hand with six fingers and a longer thumb with three joints. His face remoulded itself over broader bones, his sealed eyes tilted and lengthened.

Asleep, Bond became a strange creature shrunken in his suit of many pockets. The continuous signal which his pulse transmitted to the School now showed up on their screens as a slower, more even line of light than it had been during his troubled day.

Part Two

10. Other Patterns

In the school beyond the moon a winged figure sat beside a flat bed on which Solita lay, her hands folded on her chest. Her hair, which was deep blue in colour and looked more like long fur than human hair, was partially obscured by an object that sometimes looked like a helmet of frosted glass, and at other times appeared to be a ring of rainbow-coloured light. The winged figure held an instrument in his hand and watched a small light as it throbbed steadily on the round dial.

Glancing up at a screen above Solita's head, he spoke. "Was it necessary to involve the young child?"

"The boy will not be harmed," said the voice of the teacher. The screen shone with a variety of colours. The shapes that came and went were much more intricate than those Bond had observed when he talked to his teacher. "But Bond must realize that broken rules have direct results. The circumstances have become most interesting. We forbid excessive interaction with the inhabitants and yet our richest learning takes place when such interaction is involved."

"I did not expect such innovation," commented the winged Galgonquan. He turned to the comatose figure. "Solita. What is the present situation?"

"Speed and distance," Solita replied without opening her eyes. "The coordinates alter continuously. The Wirdegen would have lost contact had they not recruited a spy."

"The pursuers will have to make a jump if they are shaken off," the teacher observed. "That could be critical. See how a small deviation such as accepting help willingly offered, can lead to other more difficult modifications?"

"Pinpoint the coordinates when possible," the winged figure commanded Solita. "Is there any reference or name that we can check on?"

"Rackham Rides," Solita said immediately. "And Webster's Valley," she added after a pause.

"Ah, yes. We have collected other students there. That may be why the inhabitants believe it to be haunted. There have been some unfortunate instances in the past."

On the bed Solita stirred, and when her lips moved a voice issued that was not her own. "Not Webster's Valley! Everyone knows it's haunted. The trees change places," said Dora's voice in the School beyond the moon.

★　　★　　★

"The trees change places," said Koro in 1838.

"It's the shortest route," Sebastian Webster said. He barely noticed the stone tug at his ear.

They walked along a wooded ridge surrounded by the dark, rich smell of the live, green leaves and the thick, damp mulch piled up under banks of fern and moss. An unseen creek made a faint, melancholy sound below them, and a little native fantail perched pertly on a branch above their heads, chirped cheekily as it danced a little on the twig, then swooped down so low they could have touched it.

"Tenaa, Wehipa," said Hakiaha. "You tell me – how can one man think he owns all the land?" He was thinking of the landowner and the farm they had left behind them.

"I'm not like that myself," countered Sebastian, very aware of his fair hair and blue eyes. "I used to be a sailor. I don't put up any fences."

But Hakiaha looked at him doubtfully, and Sebastian Webster felt the division between them as a distinct chilliness – all the more because he knew that even if he did not erect fences other white men would, and he was frightened that he might find himself on one side of the fence, with Koro and Hakiaha on the other.

11. A Valley of Ghosts

At first the horses moved in single file, zig-zagging backwards and forwards along a track which looked like a thin thread cobbling the cleft hillside together. Divided by a gully of dense native bush, the hill looked as if it had once been struck by the wand of a powerful magician and had never recovered from the blow. The riders were surrounded by trees and ferns. Unexpected clearings showed ranks of trees climbing up and down the slopes, uneven drifts of their own fallen leaves spread across their twisted, mossy toes. The path ahead was wide enough for a horse to travel comfortably as the low branches had been trimmed back, but the bright, sharp sunlight of the world beyond the living canopy became softer by the time it reached the forest floor.

Not very far behind them were the paved yards of Rackham Rides, the office with its filing cabinet, the Range Rover and all the things that clearly proved that humankind controlled the world. And further beyond was the city, and in the city the new house which now seemed like a memory of long ago, though they had left it only that morning. The bush closed densely around them as if it must stretch out to infinity, and it was easy to believe that they had passed into a world with no other people but themselves.

Philippa sat astride a solid, black gelding called Blackberry, who would sometimes kick out if he sensed another horse close behind him on the track. A slight distance back rode David who was mounted on a large, hairy, good-natured horse called Enchanter, and Lewis on Tommy, a round, greedy pony which moved busily down the track, looking yearningly from side to side at the grass rather as if he was shopping in a supermarket. Lewis smiled as he rode, entirely wrapped in his own thoughts. Every so often he turned to check that Bond was still safely behind him riding Scoot, while beside Bond rode Dora, wearing her best blue shirt and corduroy trousers, on a horse called Prince. At the end of the line in a position she had chosen for herself, came Jake, hunched and silent, looking strangely vulnerable and small without her cowboy hat. Her horse, a pretty chestnut named Cooney, looked particularly large and powerful in contrast with Jake who looked unexpectedly defenceless in her black riding cap.

"Are you all right, Lewis?" Philippa called back a little anxiously. "You're unusually quiet this morning."

"I'm just thinking," said Lewis in an injured tone. "I'm allowed to."

Spread out like this it was easy to ride in silence, and Lewis was not the only one who was thinking private thoughts. David was still a little suspicious about the sudden decision to come on the trek, and wondered whether Dora and Jake were enjoying themselves. He wondered too about the mysterious Bond who had appeared so very early this morning, resplendent in his clothes of patches and pockets, with his scarlet hair and what looked like hundreds of dollars of electronic equipment looped around his neck. It is difficult to look at someone riding behind you, and David was trying to work out a way of watching Bond surreptitiously as he was a riddle that required solving. Meanwhile Dora considered the adventure story she was actually living, while at the rear of the group Jake was troubled about something she could not bring herself to mention.

And I'm the heroine! Dora was thinking. *I'm the one who saved Bond when he was being chased. Jake may understand what he's talking about, but I'm the rescuer!*

Poised uneasily on Cooney, Jake watched his ears, hoping they might somehow signal what his next move would be. If the right one flicked, did that mean he was going to turn to the right, she wondered? She hung on to the front of the saddle covertly until he felt reassured, and hoped Dora hadn't noticed. *Don't fall off or I'll never forgive you*, she threatened herself. *You'll be chained out in the desert covered in honey so the ants will come and eat you*. She often tried to frighten herself into a state of courage. *Me against the world!* she thought and felt better, even though riding was turning out to be a whole lot harder than it looked on television. Cooncy's back seemed to be designed for a differently shaped bottom than hers. She felt as though she was straddling a huge barrel. Yet mixed with the discomfort and the anxiety was the beginning of pleasure, for after all, she was actually sitting on a horse's back, moving forward; she was actually – yes, she was actually riding. The bush around about was green and shadowy and smelt rich – and just a little bit peppery. A bellbird called in its strange, pure voice, like a music box gone slightly wrong. Then it made a sterner, husky sound.

"It's clearing it's throat," Philippa remarked to Lewis, still worried about his silence. He slowly turned his eyes to look at her, as if he was surprised to see that there was anyone nearby, and almost as if he was unsure who was speaking.

"Wakey wakey, dreamy! Having a nice time?" Philippa asked, even more concerned by his bewilderment.

"Terrific!" said Lewis. His voice sounded higher than usual – higher and colder. The bellbird, clearing its throat again, now seemed to be making a more human sound than Lewis. It was as if they had swapped over.

Suddenly there was another bird call, and this one sounded like someone laughing. *It's laughing at me!* thought Jake. *It knows that everyone thinks I can ride.* David's parting words to her when he had last seen her over a year ago had been about horses.

"Sweetheart, you'll love it out in the country.

Your granny is a dear, even if she does blame me for everything, and there'll be Pet's horses for you to ride. You'll be better off with the horses than with me – at least until I get my life reorganized."

And now David was settled and Jake was saddled with a lot of imaginary horses. She felt them trotting invisibly alongside her, sneering with their yellow teeth, angry at being called into half-life and never truly ridden. *At least if they stand on my foot it doesn't hurt,* she thought, recalling how agonizing it was when Cooney stood on her foot back at the stables before the ride. In the shadows of the bush she smiled a little at her thoughts.

Surrounded by the shaggy bark of manuka trees, their tiny leaves speckling the air above, the riders continued in single file. Shortly however they came out onto a hunched shoulder of rock and grass that protruded from the bush making enough room for them all to gather in a group, to look across the tree tops falling away with the slope below them, and to see not only a vast sky, but also the open valley beyond.

"We'll be able to canter when we get down there," said Philippa pointing to Webster's Valley. The bird sang again. It was surprising that anything so clear and simple could also be eerie, but it was partly the great clarity that made it ghostly in a world where everything else was softened and blurred with shadows.

"Is it really haunted?" asked Jake.

"Not here," replied Philippa, "but where we're

heading – Webster's Valley – that's supposed to be haunted. Not that I've ever seen a ghost there myself, but I know all about it. A man called Sebastian Webster saw ghosts sometime during the 1830s. He wrote about it. You'll find it in the New Zealand Room at the Library – it's called 'An Account of Strange Appearances in the New Zealand Forest, by Sebastian Webster, Sailor and Whaler and Pakeha Maori'.

"What a title!" commented David. "But what was Sebastian Webster, Sailor and Whaler, doing here during the 1830s?"

"He came out to New Zealand to work on the whaling boats and ended up living with the Maoris," Philippa said, turning her head so that her voice would carry to the children behind her. "He had a Maori wife and family – there are still Websters living over the hill. Anyhow, he was coming home through this valley one day with two of his Maori friends – they'd been visiting the whaling station further around the coast and had stopped off to help the Martins at Martins Bay do a bit of pit-sawing – and they actually saw – well, Sebastian Webster said they saw ghosts."

"There's no such thing," said Jake scornfully. "Must have been shadows they saw."

"Well, I don't think it was quite as simple as that," Philippa answered. "He says they were walking home from Martins Bay when there was an earthquake – okay, nothing very strange so far. But he maintained that after the earthquake they could no longer find their way through the bush.

Everything had altered and they got lost. Then there was another earthquake and after that, suddenly, pitch black night! They blundered about, very frightened by what was happening and eventually came across a lighted glade full of mannikins and imps. Some had wings and one was blue, there was one in the shape of a horse, and all of them were outlined in silver fire."

"I'd die if I saw a ghost," said Dora sombrely. "I believe in ghosts. I'm inhibited."

"You mean 'intuitive'," Philippa corrected her. "Sebastian says the mannikins argued amongst themselves — at least their lips moved although he couldn't hear any sound. However he says his earring protected him — I think it was his earring — some charm the Maoris had given him, anyway. The ghosts took fright and vanished in a fountain of fire. Now, you have to admit that's more than shadows, Jake!"

"Sebastian Webster was a sort of great-great-uncle of my father's," added Dora, importantly. "This greenstone I'm wearing is called Wehipa's stone. Dad gave it to me for my tenth birthday. It used to be a Maori stone."

"Do you think it will keep the ghosts away?" asked Jake in a sinister voice.

Dora did not want to hear about ghosts, and she certainly did not want to see any. Once again, things were becoming too much like a horror story for her liking. As for Jake, she was far more frightened of Cooney, who was sidling towards the edge of the track. Whenever he had to step down to a lower level he seemed to vanish in front of her. It was like being stuck on top of a Ferris wheel, with nothing in front of you but space, out and down.

Lewis listened to the story of the ghosts and suddenly began to feel frightened again – not frightened of ghosts, but of the spirit that he could feel in his head. *Hello*, he said cautiously, not with his voice but with his thoughts. There was no reply but he knew someone or something was there – using his eyes to see with, making him turn his head to watch Bond from time to time, and waiting for the right moment to act. He could feel the fear as it built up in his mind, rather as if he was feeling it for another boy not for himself at all. However his companion was a fear-eater and it swallowed up the fear before Lewis had time to react. For a brief moment, however, it had begun to show on his face and Philippa noticed it, though she assumed it was the talk of the haunted bush that had scared him.

"I've ridden through the valley a thousand times," she said to comfort him, "and I've never ever seen any fading, fighting ghosts, no blue mannikins outlined in fire – nothing. Some people do say that at times the trees change places but I can't say I've noticed that either."

Dora decided to change the subject. She turned to Bond and said in a dreamy voice that made both David and Philippa sigh in despair, "I love the bush. I'd like to live here with the birds and ferns and things."

"And the wetas!" added Jake, gleefully. Dora shuddered, but Bond hesitated and looked questioningly at Jake as though he was unsure what wetas were. "They're large, brown, shiny, spiky, crawly insects with big heads," said Jake with relish, and added, "They're pretty harmless, really, but they're awfully ugly and when you try to brush them off they latch on pretty tightly."

"Well, they scare me!" said David, and Dora looked at him gratefully.

They rode on and soon came out of the bush into a long valley green with autumn grass but curiously desolate. At some time in the past someone had burnt all the bush that covered it and the valley sides were studded with a ghostly army of blackened tree stumps. These remains of taller trees than those they had just passed through looked sad against the grazing green that had taken the place of native forest. It was almost like riding into a ruined city, moving through its bleached, burnt and splintered foundations. Those parts of the tree stumps undamaged by fire had been turned silver by time and were covered with a tracery of parallel lines, thin cracks in the dried wood.

"Can you get anything on your transistor here?" Philippa asked Bond curiously, somewhat disapproving of a boy who rode with one ear continually plugged into such an expensive toy. "I should think the hills would interfere with the reception."

"Oh no, no problem at all," replied Bond. Scoot stood passively, twitching his ears as they spoke.

"He is behaving well," observed Philippa. "Scoot's often a bit naughty. You must have a way with horses."

"Do you know them all?" Bond asked. Philippa was surprised at the intent way in which he gazed at everything.

"Years ago I used to take treks out myself. That's why they let me take you lot on our own." She turned to Lewis, a slight frown creasing her forehead. "You're so quiet, Lewie. Are you feeling all right?"

Lewis smiled. He looked as if he was just waking up, and his smile was slightly fuzzy. "I was just thinking."

"Thinking again! Are you *sure* you're all right?" Philippa persisted, still puzzled by his odd behaviour. "You haven't got a headache?" But it was she who suddenly exclaimed and put a hand to her own head as she was struck by a sudden sensation. Not only Philippa but everyone else felt it too. They each cried out involuntarily and looked about in confusion. "What was that?" Philippa asked. "It felt like an electric shock!"

"Like snakes in the head," Dora cried.

"Snakes in the stomach!" David declared. It was true. There had been something snake-like in the churning twist that had overtaken them. Philippa and Dora had put their hands to their heads; David had clasped his stomach; Jake had put her hands over her ears.

"What on earth could it have been, hitting us like that?" asked Philippa, bewildered. "A mild kind of lightning?" She looked up at the sky to see the sun shining against a brilliant blue background dotted with fluffy, white clouds.

"Whoever heard of mild lightning!" said David, still very startled. "I've absolutely no idea what it could possibly have been. Was the sun out a moment ago?" Confused, everyone looked at him then gazed skywards once again.

"There are a few clouds. Well, it probably just came out from behind a cloud," suggested Jake.

"But it changed so suddenly!" Philippa exclaimed. "I know what David's getting at, I think. One moment behind a cloud, the next absolutely bright. Besides, come to think of it, I'm sure I saw the sun go under that cloud just a moment ago. Now it's going to go under it again." Everyone continued to stare into the sky suspiciously – or almost everyone. David and Dora both noticed Bond hang his head, rather as if he did not wish anyone to read his expression.

The world looked still and green and completely innocent. Dora seemed to shake herself. "Let's trot for a bit," she suggested. "We're allowed to trot here, it's a good place for it. Can we canter?"

"I'll come with you," said Philippa. "How about you, Jake? Cooney loves a canter just here." She took off effortlessly, with Dora following on immediately, and Lewis following Dora – but looking back at Bond as if he was reluctant to leave him behind. To her horror Jake saw Cooney's ears go forwards. Within moments he set off in a trot, unwilling to let the others go without him. For the terrified Jake, it was the most uncomfortable jolting movement she had ever felt. She and Cooney seemed to be acting in opposition to one another.

"Off you go!" said her father smiling as she trotted past him. He was sure she was just longing for the freedom to canter Cooney, to gallop him.

With each jolt, Jake felt one of her legs seem to grow longer than the other – she was sliding sideways in the saddle. Then at once the pace changed. Cooney was cantering. Jake thought she would dissolve with fear as she slipped still further sideways. Her right foot had come out of the stirrup and she had nothing on that side to brace herself against. She tried to cling on with her legs. In books people controlled horses and made them do what they wanted just using their hands and legs. But Jake's legs were like stuffed stockings sewn onto the edge of her jacket, with no power, no strength in them at all.

Jake pulled desperately on the reins. Cooney turned his head sideways, opening his mouth crossly, but continued to move obstinately forward. Then he slowed to a trot again. Jake had time to think that if ever she was being machine-gunned by gangsters it would be rather like this. She pulled on the reins again, but she was not dealing with an idea – Cooney was a powerful animal with likes and dislikes of his own. He did not want to stop, but when she fell forward and clung about his neck she did at least confuse him, and he got slower and slower until he at last slowed to a walk, his ears flicking bad-temperedly with disappointment. He neighed to Scoot who neighed back at him. Jake, tilted almost horizontally in the saddle, straightened herself and regained her lost stirrup. She felt dazed and shocked and her body was limp and sore. The ride had sandpapered the insides of her legs. However she had not fallen off and was quite boneless with relief at feeling in charge again (at least a little bit), and at no longer being a piece of jolting baggage, bumping along on an irritated horse. The surrounding scarred tree trunks looked calmly down at her. The riders on ahead had not seen her and the valley did not care.

"Jake!" said a voice beside her, and she looked around to find Bond staring at her. "Jake, you can't ride," he said bluntly. "They said you could ride well but you can't ride at all."

Because he simply stated the facts, without asking for an explanation, Jake didn't bother to argue. She sat motionless, thinking that whether she could ride or not, she was still entitled to dress as if she did, because they were the clothes of adventure, and once you gave difficult or even sad things the name of adventure their meaning changed.

Then Jake had a very strange experience. She felt Bond move, not in the outside world, but inside her mind. He began as a single light like a candle flame in a dark hall, investigating one side door then another, branching out and out again.

She could trace his movement in the dark land behind her eyes as if he had taken root and grown there like a tree of fire. He divided and this division divided again and again, lighting up dark places, gently searching her memories. Then he was gone — she was alone again. Bond sat beside her on Scoot studying her with a kindly interest.

"Fear is a sort of electricity and I can follow electrical traces," he told her. "I can make pictures of them when I untangle them. And now you know *my* secret too. I'm not supposed to tell anyone," he added. In reading her, in becoming a fiery tree, a river of fire flowing through her head, Bond had allowed Jake to discover something astounding about himself that she had not been able to see before.

"You're not a real person — you're — you're — you're an *alien!*" Jake blurted out at last. "You come from outer space!"

"What's 'outer space'?" asked Bond smiling. "A centimetre in front of your eyes — that's where it begins — half a centimetre, a millimetre! And what's an alien?" Bond continued, watching the others who were now riding towards them. "It's just a word for a person out of their own environment. I'm out of my place here, but you are out of yours too. You're a stranger here, just like me."

"I haven't got a place," Jake said quietly.

"Yes, you have," countered Bond. "I know you have to be the man of the family when you're at home with your mother, but here you can let yourself be a daughter."

He turned his head, and Jake saw David drawing alongside of them on his horse, a startled expression on his face as if only now was he really beginning to recognize her. He opened his mouth to speak then glanced at Bond and fell silent as the rest of the party trotted back towards them.

"It was lovely," cried Dora, forgetting to worry about what Bond was thinking of her. "Why didn't you come, Jake? I suppose it's nothing very exciting for you."

"I don't think that's quite the case," said David slowly. "But never mind. Let's just box on and enjoy the day's outing together."

Jake looked back at Bond. Now that she had got over her shock she noticed him more clearly and thought he looked pale and sad and rather frightened. "Snakes in the head!" she whispered. "The sun stepped back in the sky! Are you being followed?"

"I'm afraid so," said Bond. Lewis looked at him too but said nothing.

For a brief instant a smile flashed across his face — a smile that was not altogether his own.

12. The Vanishing of Bond

They rode on following sheeptracks in a leisurely manner, up over gradual slopes of tussocky grass interspersed with the odd broom bush. As they moved, the slopes seemed to revolve around them very slowly, opening and closing like the pages of fold-out books, every now and then revealing long valleys of bush or – through long clefts, scars of erosion – bright turquoise triangular views of the sea. The group was able to spread out. Dora and Philippa trotted away once more, pleased to have the slow descent over and done with. Jake hung back and felt the pressure of David's curious stare. Bond gave her a gentle smile then rode on ahead with Lewis trailing along behind.

Jake looked after them, contemplating something which had been happening since yesterday but which she had only just recognized. She was no longer alone. She was part of a group which had Bond as its focus. The family, which had seemed at first to consist of David, Philippa and her children, with Jake clumsily attached like the tail pinned to a party donkey, had shifted and divided into those who knew about Bond and those who didn't. Adults on one side and children on the other.

Children might believe, as Jake now believed, that Bond was a boy from outer space who was being pursued by enemies. Adults could not believe such a thing. If they did, the world would be changed too much for them to bear. And if they were forced to believe it they would then become interested not in Bond himself, but in what he might know. How did he come to be here, and why? She herself was suddenly anxious to know the strange things that Bond must know – she was burning to be told what sort of world he belonged to and what his purpose was on her world.

David, also hanging back, had fixed Jake with his glittering eye like the ancient mariner, not wanting to *tell* her a story, but to hear the one she had to tell. She tried not to look at him but he drew alongside anyway, Enchanter snorting at Cooney as if even the horses had secrets to exchange.

"If you watch me," her father said, "you'll see that you don't have to hold the reins as if you were Hercules strangling snakes. Hold them like this." Jake looked sideways at his hands. "You can't ride," he said. "I watched when you nearly fell off, but over and above that – you just can't ride."

Jake looked up defiantly. "No," she said. "Mum's horses were all sold and she didn't bother to get any more. They take a lot of looking after, horses."

"In your letters –" David began.

"I was telling lies," Jake broke in stiffly. "Why?"

Jake sighed deeply.

"Why?" David asked again, but still she would not answer. "Are you unhappy at home? Is something wrong with Pet or your grandparents?" David persisted, looking more and more dismayed, while Jake glanced from side to side out beyond the hills as if searching for a way to escape. Her face expressed the impossibility of discussing such great and complicated imperfections whilst sitting astride a horse.

Just then the others appeared, trotting back to meet them, laughing, having obviously enjoyed their small excursion.

"You sounded so happy in your letters," said David, perplexed. "All the riding —" he drifted off. "Oh Jacqueline," he said and shook his head.

"Mum reads my letters," said Jake, dropping her gaze to the reins lying limply in her hands. "She likes me to sound happy. I wanted you to think I was happy. I am sort of happy most of the time." She glanced fleetingly up at David as if she was frightened of his reaction to what she was telling him. "Nothing's ever perfect, is it?"

"Jake?" called Dora across the clearing. "We're going to stop soon and have a rest," she said, her voice loaded with hidden meaning.

"All right, off you go!" David said to Jake. "I'll catch up with you later. How *is* Pet, by the way?" he said suddenly, which wasn't quite fair. He was looking at Jake with his sad-monkey expression, as if she was the cause of his unhappiness — but after all, she thought, he was the one who had told her to go and live in a land of wonderful horses and had then gone off and got married without even asking her to the wedding.

"She likes to be looked after," she said cautiously, and David sighed.

"She always has," he said and turned away. By now the others had gathered around them, talking and patting their horses.

"Is there any reason why we shouldn't take a break now?" asked David. "Don't we usually stop about here?"

"We certainly do. There's a rail just up ahead where we can tether the horses," said Philippa.

They rode on in silence, for they each had something to worry about. David worried about Jake and Philippa directed an occasional, puzzled glance at the back of Lewis's head, and they were all still ringing a little with the 'mild lightning'. Now her secret was out, Jake felt a bit better about her lack of riding skill and was determined to improve. She tried to make Cooney catch up with the others without actually trotting again. However her efforts to encourage him to go a little faster were so timid and uncertain that he ignored them contemptuously, even insisting on putting his head down every now and then to snatch at some grass.

"How come *you* can ride?" she hissed at Bond. "Do you ride in your . . . where you come from?"

"I have a way with animals," he said. "I can control them — but we're not supposed to, and we must never, never control people. Not that I can do people. I'm only a student."

"Even now if you're being followed?" asked Jake. "Couldn't you control the ones that are after you?"

"I may be being followed but I can't feel anyone close and neither can —" He broke off and laid his hand on his transistor. "The world's quite empty."

Dora came up beside them. "Bond says he's being followed," Jake told her. Dora gazed around. The line of the hills against the sky was entirely empty. Nothing moved on the track behind them.

"There's nobody there," she said. "They couldn't be ahead of us."

"I don't know what to do," Bond said. He was talking aloud, but not to Dora or Jake.

"We'll look after you," Dora promised him.

They rode out along a flattened ridge which fell away on either side into deep bush. The sound of water came faintly to their ears, for somewhere below them hidden among the trees was a stream that must, by the sound of it, be flowing over stones.

"Webster's Bush," announced Philippa. "There are the tethering rails. We'll take a break here."

"It does look haunted," Dora said, staring uneasily down the slope at the dense, green, uneven canopy of trees below them. They dismounted and Philippa went from one to the other checking that they put the stirrups up correctly.

Lewis let Philippa do the task for him. "You know how to do this, Lewis!" she said. "Come on — shake out of it!"

"I don't remember," said Lewis in a composed, but slightly childish voice.

"You do!" Philippa exclaimed. "You must. What's wrong with you today?"

"I'm fine," he replied. "Really I am. It isn't my fault if I forget. It's eagle weather. I'm looking with my eagle eyes and my eagle claws can't do up stirrups."

"Aaah, I see," Philippa looked relieved. "Dream on, you old eagle you!"

As soon as they stopped talking they were engulfed in a sunny silence, not hostile, but not exactly welcoming either. It was as if the hills did not mind them being there but would not mind if they went away. Jake thought it was very restful. Lewis, having been firmly summoned by Philippa, became quite interested in the tea, orange juice and biscuits that were being offered and forgot all about Bond for a few minutes. Dora jiggled from one foot to the other watching the tea being poured. She really preferred orange juice, but on the other hand, tea would be warm and comforting. She felt her stomach glow a little with anticipation.

"Have some tea, Bond," she called as she turned around, looked once, looked again, and then immediately felt her stomach grow cold once more. There was only one person behind her – Jake, forlorn without her cowboy hat prop. Dora moved away from her chattering parents to Jake's side. " Bond's gone," she muttered. "I just turned around and he wasn't there anymore."

Jake looked over her shoulder. She had imagined Bond would be standing with Lewis and Dora drinking some orange juice and being almost normal - but it was true, he was gone. She could see the horses tied to their rail, she could see the slope beyond rising up to touch a pale blue sky, but Dora was right. There was no Bond.

"He might have gone off for a moment to – you know!" suggested Jake. Dora was horrified. Somehow she could never bring herself to believe that beautiful people might even actually need to go to the lavatory.

"Do you think so?" she asked Jake trustingly. She had come to realize that because someone looked like the Lone Ranger it didn't mean they couldn't think carefully.

"We'll wait a minute, just in case," advised Jake, "but I don't really think that's it. I think it might have something to do with the electric snakes."

"The mild lightning," Dora corrected her, not relishing the thought of electric snakes. "Suppose he has gone? What will we do?"

Jake did not answer at once. She did not know. She found herself thinking that Bond had become so strange and such a responsibility that there was a sort of temptation to let him simply vanish from their lives. But that was being cowardly again. She simply shrugged and said, "Perhaps Lewis has seen him."

Philippa sipped her hot tea and glanced over at

the two girls. "They seem to be getting on just fine," she said. David nodded hopefully. As parents they were so involved with their own various family difficulties that they did not notice that Bond was missing.

13. Up the Creek

"He's gone," Jake said. "Bond's gone."

"Gone?" repeated Lewis looking very distressed. "Which way?"

"He said he was being followed," said Dora, "but there's no-one else around."

"At least he hasn't taken his horse," commented Jake. "Perhaps if he really wants to go, we should let . . . " She trailed off under Dora's reproachful stare.

Webster's Bush, lapping like the tide below them, had swallowed up Bond. He must have simply got off his horse and walked off without the slightest hesitation into the shadows. Now there was only the bush looking back at them, dense and silent, not giving away any secrets. The clearing spread out behind them to the lip of the valley of ruined trees and made way for the sky. On either side of them it fell away into Webster's Valley.

"He might be playing a joke," said Jake doubtfully, not believing it for a second. Bond didn't possess that sort of playfulness, and besides, he just didn't understand how impossible it was too walk away into thin air. Soon the time would come for them to ride on. There would be an empty

113

horse and questions asked. There would be a search, confusion, and eventually tempers would be frayed. If he was still not found, perhaps a bigger search would be organized – helicopters, and policemen with dogs. There was no way that David and Philippa would just ride back home not bothering about where he had gone, leaving Bond forgotten and lost to the world.

"I think he's gone down to the creek," said Dora decisively. "In the bush the creek would act as a sort of road. He'd go down till he reached the creek and then walk along it."

Jake agreed that this was quite probable but just where had he gone into the bush? She looked from one side to the other, biting her thumbnail.

"We have to look for him," hissed Lewis. "We must find him." He sounded extremely upset, almost hysterical, as if he was the one who would be blamed and punished for Bond's disappearance.

Though he kept his voice low, his anxiety was felt by Philippa who looked over at them and called, "Is everything okay, kids?"

"Yeah – we're just going to explore the bush for a little while," said Dora quickly.

"Don't go too far," said David, good-humouredly. "We'll have to move on shortly."

Jake turned to the other two. "Let's try here," muttered Jake. "If I was going into the bush, I'd go down here."

Following the sound of the creek they entered a strange, drifting, cobwebby world, but the cobwebs were actually lichen. The native beech and fuschia were trimmed with a torn, grey-green lace so delicate that its edges appeared to vanish smokily into the air. Lichen smudged the firm edges of trunk and bough.

"They're pleased we're being friendly," observed Dora.

"Who are?" asked Jake.

"Our parents. They were so busy watching how we were getting along, they didn't even notice Bond wasn't there!"

"They would've soon enough," said Jake grimly.

The three children slid down over banks heavy with fallen leaves, ferns and grasses. Branches extended like hands to touch them as they struggled by. There was no proper track, but the soft sound of the running stream was their guide.

"This is hopeless," said Jake, looking into the forest which surrounded them. "Even if we *were* on the right track we could still easily miss him."

"But we've got to try!" Lewis said, bouncing with anxiety. "I don't want Bond lost!"

"I don't want him somewhere on his own where his enemies can get at him," added Dora.

"We mightn't make much difference in that case," snorted Jake, though she knew that they were so tied to Bond that they had to find him. She could imagine the police asking her: *How long did you say you'd known this boy? Where did you meet him?* She could visualize the headlines in the newspapers and imagine the endless questioning, even as she remembered Bond's mind moving through hers like a tree of fire.

They slid down yet another bank. Dora landed on her feet, then stood motionless. "Listen!" she said. They each stopped and listened. There was a settling sound as the bush through which they had just scrambled quietened down again. But beyond that was a silence so huge that all the sounds they could hear – the voices of birds and of the stream below – accentuated it. In the city there was always a lot of noise; cars crossing and recrossing via roads and motorways, motorbikes leaping away as the lights turned green, dogs barking and radios blaring out music, while in the air planes droned like distant insects, and beyond all the noises which had names was another sound – a constant breathing made up of a thousand unnamed sounds which somehow ran together into a daylight hum, reassuring everyone that the city was still alive and working. But here, behind the bird call and the rustle of the leaves and the liquid voice of the creek below them, there was nothing but a crouching silence into which they were crashing in their search for Bond.

Lewis listened for a few seconds then pushed on anxiously. The girls could see him a few metres further down the slope, no longer as a whole boy, merely as patches of colour amidst the leaves.

"Suppose there was a spirit in the bush that would help us?" said Dora hopefully.

"There probably is," replied Jake, "but how do we make it notice us? At home it's quiet all around just like this, and I like it most of the time, but it couldn't care less about me. Oh well. Bond can't have much of a start on us."

They pressed on, following what they could see of Lewis. The babble of the creek grew louder and louder, until at last they could actually detect the movement of water. A little further on, they scrambled down another little slope to find themselves suddenly confronted by a narrow, stony stream. Lewis was slightly ahead, looking back at them.

"Here's a footprint!" he shouted excitedly, as though he had traced a clue in a birthday party treasure hunt. "Lots of them! They're full of water." He did not wait for the girls to catch up with him but moved quickly on, stalking Bond.

Moments later, Dora and Jake reached the same spot, cast a cursory glance over the footprints in the flat, muddy sand on one side of the creek, and set off after Lewis. Once around the bend the bush closed in more snugly about them and they saw a series of bush pools, turned to clouded amber by the shafts of sunlight filtering down through the trees. Entranced, the two girls picked their way carefully, pushed together by the narrowness of the creek bed, sometimes going one after the other, sometimes pressed shoulder to shoulder. Here in this deep, silent, lonely place Dora looked at Jake and found herself able to ask the questions that she had long dreamed of asking, since that time when Jake was still a long-haired promise in a photograph.

"Were you sorry when David and your mother split up?" she asked, and though she had tried to speak in a low voice, her question came out with a rough edge to it that immediately made her feel shy in that old bush silence. But Dora badly wanted to know the answer, for she understood her own life best when she compared it with other people's lives. She had always been curious about Jacqueline-in-the-photograph, whose life seemed as if it might be an unknown reflection of her own. Looking sideways she saw Jake look startled, nervous and then sort of far away, as if she was trying to remember.

"They said it had to be," she answered at last. "They said it'd be for the best – for all of us. I think David's happier but my mother isn't."

"David told Philippa your mother was the one who wanted to leave," said Dora, timid but persistent.

"I don't remember how it all happened. I was only a little kid – nine years old – and they didn't tell me a lot, or else I don't remember it if they did. They didn't get on too badly or anything, I don't think, but the happiest time for my mother was before I was born. She didn't really want to ever grow up, or become a mother and have to do all the things mothers do. But when she broke up with Dad she found out that going home to her parents was different from what she thought it would be."

"In what way?" asked Dora with trepidation, feeling water seep into her sneakers as she trod carelessly in soft sand. Although she was afraid

Jake might become angry at her questions, she couldn't contain her curiosity.

"Well, she was an only child and my gran and granddad thought she was wonderful. She was pretty too – she still is, in an old sort of way."

"Like my mother," interjected Dora, "except my mother doesn't try to make the best of herself."

"My mother's called 'Pet'. She likes that name, probably because that's what she wants to be – someone's darling pet." Jake began to speak more fiercely. "I think my Dad might have been like the man in the Curly Locks rhyme, but promised her wrongly. Anyway, she says he did."

"How does it go?" asked Dora, frowning as she tried to remember the rhyme.

"Curly Locks, Curly Locks, will you be mine? You shall not wash dishes nor yet feed the swine," quoted Jake. Dora remembered and joined in with the last two lines triumphantly,

"But sit on a cushion and sew a fine seam and feed upon strawberries, sugar and cream."

"Tracks! More tracks!" called Lewis from a point not far ahead. Dora discovered that she had completely forgotten that they were supposed to be finding Bond. The rhyme had given her a very good idea of what Jake's mother must be like.

"When I was little," continued Jake, "she used to recite that rhyme to me and she'd say, 'That's what your Daddy promised me'." Jake shrugged. "Anyhow, I don't think anyone should ever promise that – a lovely life of strawberries!"

"Only rich people could do that," said Dora,

patting her own hair to feel if it was curly enough. "Mind you, it works."

"What works?" asked Jake, bewildered.

"Curly hair! The man in the poem wouldn't have promised her strawberries and cream if her hair had been straight," said Dora as if it was beyond all doubt. "Well, not unless she had a good cut."

They had almost caught up to Lewis, but now they paused to study the footprints in the mud. "It is hard to tell – suppose they're not Bond's?" said Dora uncertainly.

"Who else would be walking here? We haven't seen or heard anybody else all day. Webster's ghosts? They don't leave prints. Ghosts don't have weight." Lewis was just a couple of metres ahead of them now and they followed on, picking their way cautiously.

"My granddad had a stroke," Jake went on after a moment. "He's not exactly crippled but he can't move around very well. He's the one who needs looking after. And my gran isn't too well either. So you see, neither of them can look after themselves properly, let alone look after Mum. Every now and then she talks as if she came home to look after them but I know she didn't. Even now she doesn't do much around the place."

Dora thought Jake's mother sounded awful, and thought how nice it must be for David to be free of her and living with Philippa and two nice children. Then she felt that since Jake was confiding in her, she should reciprocate with a confidence of her own. "My father met someone really pretty and went off with her," she offered. "He just left home one weekend."

"My mother was dreadfully upset when David married again," Jake answered. "I think she always thought he'd be there for her to go back to if things didn't work out. She cried a lot. But anyhow – not to worry! It's all over and done with now."

There was a new sound in the air. Dora thought she could hear a big truck being driven slowly over distant hills, a soft, monotonous murmur that seemed to echo. "Where are we going? How far do we follow?" she asked, looking around as if she had suddenly woken up and was surprised to find herself still walking through the forest. "How can he have got so far ahead?"

"He might be around the next corner," said Jake. "Lewis, can you see anything?" she called.

"There's a waterfall over here!" Lewis called back. He looked over his shoulder, a worried frown on his face. "Come on! I don't want Bond to get lost."

"We've come quite a long way," said Dora fretfully. "David and Mum will be wondering where we are." They turned the bend and saw the stream grow flatter and wider. High above them narrow, silver streaks of water bracketed the upper rocks then flowed together, foaming, down into the wrinkling pool in front of them. "How will we get up there?" asked Dora despairingly.

"There are plenty of rocks sticking out the side. We'll be able to climb up easily," said Jake confidently.

Lewis stood at the base of the waterfall gazing upwards, his hand resting on a mossy branch as if it was the back of some green, furry animal. Then he began to climb sure-footedly, as if he had climbed up those rocks many times before. He seemed to know instinctively where to put his feet and hands. Jake and Dora followed, one on either side of the waterfall. Suddenly Bond's voice rang out from the air above them. He was actually standing on the lip of the waterfall, looking down at them.

"Don't follow me!" he cried desperately. "Let me go away and don't follow me. I am followed by too many already. I should never have let you help me. Don't follow!"

"Who *is* following you?" asked Dora. "You said that before but no-one was following you. I looked everywhere. There was no-one there."

"Remember the jump?" he asked mysteriously. "You felt them move closer. They made time shrug." He looked at their blank faces. "Never mind. You don't understand."

"You don't understand either," Jake threw back at him. "If you go away now, people will search for you – our people, that is – and they won't stop looking until they find some trace of you." As she spoke she stopped climbing, growing rigid with amazement and fear. Behind Bond, but still on the rock lip over which the water plunged turning white then silver and then clear as glass as it flowed through a long patch of sunlight, three black patches were forming in mid-air taking on the rough shape of men. They were flat and black, like figures in a shadow theatre but they seemed to be filling out somehow. It was as though something was rushing into them from somewhere and Jake felt that in a moment they would have texture and substance. Right now, however, they looked as if they had been burnt into the air, and that anything that poured *into* them could also gush out *through* them and flood onlookers with blackness.

A quivering began, not only in the air but in the actual rocks under their hands and feet. It was not quite an earthquake – living as they did in an area prone to earthquakes, Jake and Dora were both familiar with the sensation and were vaguely aware that this movement was too mathematical to be an earthquake. It was as if someone had plucked an invisible string in the very heart of all matter, and now the entire world was vibrating to a single note. The figures moved and stretched out black shapes that were not quite real hands. They could not seize anything yet, but were getting ready to do so. They were preparing to take Bond. Lewis said nothing, but Dora screamed in horror.

"Bond! Watch out!"

"Where?" he asked.

"Behind you! Behind you!" Dora cried.

Bond turned, saw them, and spoke in a different voice and a different language while at the same time desperately dragging at the box under his arm, fumbling with the transistor switches. In an instant there came a sound as penetrating as a needle thrust in at the ear, dissolving into the blood, and coursing like a thousand little needles around the body. The black figures suddenly broke up into black rags and then to a swarm of swirling fragments before vanishing completely. Jake stared at this scene in terror. Dora, looking up towards Lewis, saw his hands grow limp and begin to slide away from the stone. She cried out as she felt him fall like a heavy bundle past her, down the rocky outcrop at the side of the waterfall, crashing to the ground below.

14. A Jump Into the Past

Back on the ridge David and Philippa, angry and puzzled at the lengthy disappearance of their patchwork family, felt the world flicker and then for a terrifying moment they felt completely disoriented.

"What on earth —" David began, but Philippa interrupted.

"David, don't try and think about it. Don't try and work it out. Let's just concentrate on what to do next."

"The horses . . ." David said. "Oh, no!"

"The children . . ." said Philippa, her face pale and stricken.

In spite of their concern they did nothing immediately except fling their arms about each other and bury their faces in each other's shoulder, giving them a much-needed moment of darkness and closeness in which to get used to the fantastic alteration of their environment.

"Electric snakes!" breathed David faintly at last, followed by "Good heavens!" Philippa felt for his hand and twisted her fingers into his before opening her eyes.

They were still at their picnic place and it was open to the sky, but the whole forest had somehow crept up from below. The rail to which the horses had been tied had disappeared, and the horses themselves stood oddly among the trees of a forest that had never known horses. Enchanter and Scoot, who had fallen onto their sides, scrambled clumsily to their feet. It was no longer possible to look down onto the bush and see it as something over which people had control, for it now towered above them, as if in a single second they had slept for a hundred years and had woken to find seeds had sprouted into huge, old trees. There was evidence of man's habitation as someone had been working on the ridge, clearing a space – the wood of several tree stumps was still white and clean, unweathered by the elements. Every fern, every leaf and every twig seemed to stand out as though it was outlined with a thread of silver. There was a crashing sound – Cooney, contrary as ever, plunged away into the imposing forest that surrounded them.

"It's impossible," Philippa said. Her teeth chattered as she spoke but she was not cold. David said nothing for a moment. When he spoke at last, he was shivering too.

"Something very strange has happened," he muttered. "I don't think we can afford to think about it too much. I mean – we could go mad just trying to understand it. We'll just do what we've got to do – look for the kids."

"Yes," agreed Philippa. She smiled weakly and added, "I'm so frightened my legs have stopped working!"

"Mine too!" replied David. "Hug me and make me strong." They embraced once more.

As David and Philippa embraced, down by the waterfall the quivering stopped. Jake still clung steadfastly to the rocks, her eyes squeezed firmly shut. When she opened them again she saw that her eight fingertips were yellowish-white and her nails were almost white too. Their usual pinkness had shrunk to a patch in the middle of each nail because she had been hanging on so tightly. Next she found to her surprise and disgust that she had been a little sick, and her mouth tasted of the orange drink she had drunk only a short time before, now sour and bitter. Someone seized her wrists. It was Bond. There were actual tears on his cheeks, tears so recently wept they were still moving.

"I'm sorry," he sobbed. "I didn't want this to happen. I'm so confused, I – " he stopped talking as he felt her come alive again and take control of her hands, grasping the rock anew, though still blinking and dazed.

"Dora!" she called. "Dora! Are you all right?"

"I slid down a bit," wailed Dora. "My knees will be all scraped." She directed herself at Bond. "What did you do? Where's Lewis?"

"I'm all right now," said Jake as Bond climbed down past her towards Dora. She began to climb back down herself, and a moment later stood at the foot of the waterfall beside the immobile form of Lewis, while Bond helped Dora down the last little bit of the rock face.

Jake could see at once that Lewis was alive, though she was reminded in a horrid way of a broken toy. He was breathing deeply and evenly. Dora burst into tears and wailed aloud. Jake now realized that Dora's noisy cries were because she needed to talk, squeak, whimper – anything to keep herself on the move. Dora's own sound was like a drum for her to march to. So Dora cried loudly, and Jake was silent, but each in their own way was trying to cope with the difficult circumstances.

"Is it all right to move Lewis?" Jake asked Bond. "He might have broken bones. Can you tell?"

"Solita?" Bond looked into the air questioningly. Jake thought he was swearing in his alien language.

"He is alive and well," replied Solita, but neither Jake nor Dora could hear her. "It is very strange. He must have been unusually susceptible. We have driven them off but not very far. I can still feel them hovering but now I need to recharge. So will they, I think, unless they have a great reserve of power on which to draw."

"He's all right – just stunned," Bond reported to the two girls. "Help me lift him out of the mud." Jake hesitated. "I promise it won't hurt him," Bond assured her. Together they gently laid Lewis on the carpet of dried leaves and grass to the side of the stream.

"He's fainted," said Dora. "Mum'll know what to do. We'll make a stretcher with our coats like we learned in First Aid, and carry him home." She pictured herself, frail but brave, caring only for her little brother, her hair wonderfully curly in spite of the single smudge of dirt on her flower-like cheek.

Jake noticed Dora was dreaming again. "Wakey, wakey!" she said gently. Jake's breathing had altered and she was now panting slightly. She was afraid. "We don't even know where we are anymore."

From the few glimpses of the world she had had as she stumbled to Lewis's side, Dora already knew things had changed but that was something she could not bear to think about. Now there was no choice. She had to listen, lift her head and look around at a world which knew nothing of pretty hair or heroic friends and sisters. Perhaps, she reflected, it knew nothing of people. Somehow the whole bank on the west side of the creek had tilted. Just for a moment Dora was convinced she must be standing side on to everything. The stream chattered more loudly than before, not because the surroundings were any quieter or because it was excited by the adventures people were having on its banks, but because it was deeper and swifter than it had been. The waterfall had grown higher and more narrow. There were still trees but no longer the same trees. The silence beyond the sound of the stream was the same silence however, ancient and enchanted. Their voices crawled in it like little insects in the silence of an endless, shadowy hall.

They were all aliens together now in a place that belonged to none of them. Dora noticed that the trees, the leaves and the ferns appeared as though someone had scratched around them with a pin of light. Jake's teeth chattered slightly as if she was cold but it was fear she was struggling to keep clenched behind her teeth, not chilliness.

Jake turned to Bond who to her eyes stood in this world like the very spirit of the change. "What have you done to us?" she asked him accusingly. She wanted to say 'What have you got us into?' but she knew they had no-one to blame but themselves on that score — they had got themselves into it, wishing to be adventurous in the fight against evil. They had wanted to help Bond, to be daring and brave . . . but had ended up unsure and afraid.

"We've gone back in time," stated Bond. "I can't tell how far. The Wirdegen made a big jump and time jumped back too."

"Gone back in time!" cried Dora and Jake together.

"I tried to warn you without actually telling you what I suspected might happen, but you wouldn't give up!" Bond said, a note of anguish in his voice. "I should have just walked away from you when I first met you, because when I did try to leave you it was already too late. Solita warned me that there was a Wirdegen presence but she couldn't tell me where. Then I felt the jump." A moment before Bond had seemed bright as a star in the shadows of the bush. Now he seemed more human — he was unhappy and that was easy to recognize even in a changed world. "All the same," he added, "I think it was fated that we should meet because of the stone."

"The stone?" asked Dora in a quivering voice.

"You've got to tell us everything now," said Jake firmly, squatting down beside Lewis, "no matter what you promised anyone else."

Bond looked up. A last, single, glassy bead clung to his cheek. Bond touched it and it vanished into a damp smear as he looked at his fingertip with interest. He even licked it. And all the time he was listening to a voice they could not hear.

"What are you listening to?" asked Dora desperately. "What do you hear through your radio?"

"It's my transistor . . . trans – sister," said Bond, smiling a little as he gave the word a different emphasis. "It's hard for you to understand."

"We're not stupid!" said Dora indignantly.

"No, Dora – it's something really strange," Jake told her. "I should have told you sooner, but forgot about it with all those questions of yours about Mum and Dad. Bond isn't from our world. He's from somewhere else."

"What do you mean?" Dora looked as if her hair might stand on end. "He's not a ghost –?"

"I'm Galgonquan," Bond answered proudly as if he expected them to know and understand. "Both of us are." Then, seeing their blank faces he disconnected the lead from his ear and pressed a switch that would enable him to hear Solita without using the ear piece. "This box may look like a radio but it holds some of the capacities and qualities of my sister, Solita who is, well, older than me. She's more advanced."

Dora and Jake looked at each other quite

baffled. "But what's it for? And what does it actually do?" asked Dora, staring at the box as if it had suddenly sprouted evil eyes and was looking at her. "And why are you here?"

"I was sent down to do my first test." Bond paused doubtfully. "We all have to do a test at different times."

"A sort of exam?" offered Jake. He frowned over the word then suddenly seemed to understand.

"Yes," he replied. "It is very much the same. I did the first part well enough I think, but then I came up against a Wirdegen unit – but you wouldn't know what a Wirdegen is, would you?"

Dora tore her anxious gaze from Lewis and glared at him. "Of course not! Why are they after you?"

"It's a bit complicated," he said, "but I'll try to simplify things for you." He did not say anything for a short space of time and the only sound was the faint, busy, warbling voice of the stream hurrying past their feet. "We Galgonqua," he said at last, "are trying to make something that is a great work of art – and of science as well. We call it the Inventory – a collection of all the knowledge in the Universe, but an integral part of knowledge is the way we connect things together. We think that when it's all put together it'll be more than a list. It will make a wonderful pattern."

"It makes you sound like a whole planet of librarians!" said Jake jokingly, and she was surprised when Bond's face lit up and he agreed with her.

"That's just it! That's what we are. We are the holders and arrangers of knowledge. We never know, or even meet, our parents as you do, but spend our life in the School travelling through the dimensions to various points in space to study – oh, everything, because everything matters, nothing is disconnected from anything else."

"Really? Nothing?" repeated Dora looking from Lewis to Bond to Jake with consternation.

"People like me come down into a society like this one – this one in particular because this is where the Galgonquan race began – and we study our surroundings and retain what we see. We sift memories and match them with other memories. We name the ways in which things fit together, we put knowledge in order and share it where it's needed. We know when things run side by side and when they cross over. We can recall information more quickly than any of your computers – it's part of our power."

"Are you our ancestors?" Dora asked incredulously.

"Descendants," Jake said quickly. "You'd be a descendant, wouldn't you, Bond?"

"In a way, but we're a mixture. We are descended from other peoples too, and we're altered by what we call 'genetic specialization'. For example, I have gills – I can breathe underwater and in very thin air."

"Can your enemies do that?" asked Jake, surreptitiously looking for his gills. Bond nodded.

"They can do most of what I can do," he explained. "We're distant cousins. There was once a community of Galgonqua called the Wirdegen. They didn't want to submit to the authority of the School. They were very bright and wonderful people and thought knowledge should be free and readily available to everyone, not given out like carefully selected prizes. Eventually, they broke away from the rest of us and set up on their own. This was many years ago. The difficulty is that we Galgonqua don't work well as individuals, not like your people do. We are interlinked, and once the Wirdegen broke off from the rest of us they slowly changed and lost their good ideas and their strength. And, as they slowly lose their powers, cooling down like a piece of burning wood which has fallen out of the main fire, they try to pirate us, steal our children and make connections through them."

He sounded as if he was absent-mindedly quoting someone as he stroked his forehead thoughtfully and stared down at Lewis's unconscious face. "The Wirdegen are pirates of knowledge," he continued. "They want to steal from the Inventory and give nothing back to it."

Lewis suddenly muttered something and threw out his arm.

"Lewis," said Dora kneeling over him, her lower lip trembling. "Wake up, Lewie, wake up!"

Jake watched Dora draw Lewis to her, wishing that she had someone to hug. She turned back to Bond. "So they caught up with you?"

"The chance of meeting the Wirdegen here was very small," Bond reflected. "They must be incredibly good at tracing, too. I could have sworn I was free. But you felt them – they made a big jump through time and space – 'teleporting' I think you call it. I can do it too but I'm forbidden to do it here because of effects like this." He indicated their surroundings with a sweeping gesture. "You see, a jump without the proper compensation messes up a lot of other things as well. Time flickers. I'm not clever enough to make the exact compensation yet, and the Wirdegen just don't bother."

At this moment Lewis stirred and looked with unfocused eyes up at Dora. "Dora," he said after a moment, "who are we chasing?"

"Lewie," she cried, beaming with relief. "We were following Bond, remember, and then his enemies appeared. Do you remember that?"

"I fell," said Lewis, concentrating hard. "I fell down, didn't I?"

"The black shapes frightened you and your fingers slipped from the rock," said Dora, for that was what she believed. Lewis looked at her seriously. He shook his head slightly and opened his mouth to speak but no words came out. "Don't try to talk," said Dora. "Just lie still for a minute."

With Lewis's return to consciousness a dreadful pressure lifted from them. In the middle of a mystery they still enjoyed an unexpected moment of ease.

"Have I got it right, then?" asked Jake. "You actually teleport and that alters time?"

"We move forward using a particular energy, and the sudden draining of this energy sends time

135

back. There *are* ways of moving where time will be unaffected but those methods have to be carefully learnt and perfected. You see, we don't altogether understand *why* it happens, and it's a mystery even to those who can do it properly. They argue about the past we drop into – is it really the past, or is it just that people are suddenly able to *see* the past and only the past? We're not sure if the jump affects the place or the way we perceive the place. But it could upset everything in a city or a town – anywhere where people live. We're lucky that we're in a lonely place. Their first jump was only a little one, it made a difference of only a second or two – remember the electric snakes? – but the second one built on the first. And if they jump again, we'll move even further back."

"Do you mean to say we're actually in the *past?*" asked Dora with dread. "I can't think of anything I could want less!"

"We may only think we are," said Bond, in a reassuring voice. "It might be that it's *us* who have altered so that we can see only the past. No-one knows for sure."

Dora stared at him in disbelief. He still looked beautiful, but his difference now showed so clearly, both in the calm manner in which he spoke, and the fact that he seemed to think he might be comforting her by saying this. She could have screamed at him. Dropping down beside Lewis again, Dora flung her arms about him. "Don't worry, Lewie," she said, as much in an effort to comfort herself as her brother. She was tremendously pleased, however, to realize that Jake was no longer an enemy, but a human being with the same thoughts and feelings as herself, the same fear, the same outrage.

"Are we stuck here forever?" Jake look at Bond questioningly. "I mean, can we get back again?" Dora was secretly pleased also to hear that Jake's voice was shaking. *Stranded in time!* rang out a voice in her mind. *Stranded in time!* "Oh, no. It's only an effect, it won't last long. It will fade," answered Bond. "You don't belong here. See how each plant is edged with light? If we were properly matched up we wouldn't see that. The further back in time, the greater that effect becomes and the wider the zone of influence. You're safe – truly. Just be patient and you'll drift back to your own time and there'll be no more trouble for you. All this is happening because you are with me."

There was a deadly hush in the old bush. As Jake and Dora helped Lewis to his feet, they understood that part of the tranquillity about them was the silence of the past. They could hear the clockwork of the years not ticking but sighing out into the quietude. Some things remained unchanged. The native fuschia still shed scrolls of bark, and the beech trees still wore the lacy grey-green of their lichen, so that the edges of their trunks were not clear-cut like those of garden trees, but faded out somewhat fuzzily into the air.

"I suppose there's not much we can do to help you now," said Jake wearily. "We should be thinking of helping ourselves. We might even get in your way."

"We won't even know what happens to you," Dora broke off suddenly. "Let's get Lewis home," she wailed, looking fearfully at their transformed world. "But how can we? Are we in a different time from Mum and David?" She looked worried.

"Different time?" asked Lewis as he sat up looking quite bewildered at the change in the trees around them. "Where's Mummy? I want to go home."

"We'll go in just a little while," Dora said, her voice trembling. "When we know where to go," she added under her breath.

"It will be all right if you just sit here," said Bond touching her on the arm in an attempt to comfort her. "Think of it as a very mysterious dream. And it *is* mysterious because I must have been drawn to meet *you*, Dora, by a very strange effect. There was what we call an 'object anomaly'. That stone you're wearing around your neck – I was wearing it too. The present form and the future one pulled towards each other, and then when I got into the car with you my stone vanished. It was the same stone you see, but in two different existences."

"My stone!" exclaimed Dora putting her hand to her throat to touch it.

"My father – my real father – gave it to me."

"My father gave me mine too – sort of," said Bond. "I came to your time – a time where it already existed – and it cancelled itself out. But first, the attraction of the two stones pulling towards each other led me to you. It's all been a wonderful experience for me, and if I get back to my School I'll have so much to tell about – riding and red hair, and unexpected friends."

Lewis started to get to his feet. Dora put her arm around his waist and helped him.

"Don't go," Dora said to Bond, but with none of her earlier determination.

"It's a bit like Captain Scott's last expedition," Jake said uneasily. "They were dying of cold and hunger in the Antarctic, and Captain Oates was getting weaker and he knew he was holding the rest of them back. So one morning he said, 'I am just going outside for a moment, gentlemen. I may be some time', and although they knew he wouldn't come back, they let him go."

Dora remembered learning about this at school, but she had always imagined being Captain Oates, not one of the people who let him go.

Lewis suddenly startled them all by crying out, "No! No, I don't want Bond to go. No! I won't let him walk into the bush." He clung furiously to Bond. "You're not to leave us."

"Wirdegen alarm! Wirdegen alarm!" Solita warned Bond.

"They're close," Bond said, trying to detach Lewis gently. "They could be in the air around us."

Jake and Dora quickly looked all around but could see nothing to be worried about. There was no sign of any living thing, with the exception of one small fantail which came darting down, zigging and zagging with its unique twitching flight, danced around on a fallen branch nearby, spoke to them in high-pitched cheeps, then shot away again like a clockwork toy suddenly released to fly free.

"It will be difficult at first," Bond told them. "Especially when the whole world begins churning and changing, but it will pass – it will settle down to a grey-green blur, night and day running together to make one twilight, whole summers nothing but little flashes of brightness."

"Like a cassette tape quickly rewinding," said Dora, inspired.

"Mmm – rather like that," Bond agreed after some hesitation, "and then the present – your time – will approach and there will be accumulated drag. The days will slow down again, and when the silver line vanishes you'll know you're back in your own time, one reality fitting exactly over another, everything matching up. You'll be back where you started and can just walk upstream to your parents. I don't know how far this distortion spreads but it may be that they won't even have missed you."

"We've been away for ages," said Dora.

"But mostly in another time!" Bond reminded her, smiling. He looked from one to the other of them. "Thank you for all you have done and all you have tried to do for me. You've been good friends and if ever I get back to my School, it will all be put down in the great Inventory to become a part of the information of the Universe. It will be part of that pattern I was talking about."

Jake and Dora watched Bond turn to go, both feeling powerless to protect either him or themselves but unable to think of any more arguments to prevent him from leaving. By now they were so overwhelmed by the silver-edged forest and by the strange things Bond had divulged, that although they felt desperate and sad at seeing him turn and walk away, they also felt a certain guilty relief.

"Have we all stopped being brave?" Dora asked Jake, who shrugged and sighed but said nothing.

"No!" shouted Lewis. He sounded shaken and weak, but desperate too.

"Bond!" commanded a voice and Bond stopped. It was a man's voice but it came from Solita, and went on to speak in a series of twitters and clicks as if a bird was trapped in the box behind the buttons and switches. "The time is now! Contact is re-established!" Solita reported. Bond stared down at the box with astonishment and relief. "Elementary Chikkulen breathing with repetition of the first Xu formula co-ordinates for voluntary metamorphose will be read to you. Walk in the direction indicated on the dial."

Bond looked back at Dora and Jake and Lewis. "Did you hear?" he cried, seizing his Companion as if it was a book, clasping it against his chest. "Did you hear what he said?"

"How could we understand?" Dora said. "It was all squeaks and clicks!" But she had understood enough, and smiled.

"I might be saved after all. I might be saved!" Bond cried. The Companion began to reel off a long list of numbers and, almost as if all living things responded to the rhythm of the voice, a ripple of movement spread through the forest.

There was the sound of a flock of frightened birds as they rose out of the tree-tops, beating their wings furiously. Change accelerated so that at one moment the trees around were sunny and peaceful in their net of silver fire, and the next they were lashing in the grip of a wind from the past which had, however, no power to ruffle Jake, Dora, Lewis or Bond. They stood in the heart of a storm but remained untouched by it. A nearby branch tore away leaving a long, ivory scar amidst the grey bark, which immediately began to discolour and heal. From somewhere up above them, another bough – a dry one – snapped so sharply that they all jumped. It fell at Jake's feet and she bent to pick it up.

"Pay attention," she urged Bond anxiously as she noticed his eyes wandering too. "Don't miss anything!"

"I am," he said, surprised. "What I'm hearing is like a mathematical password. When I have absorbed it all, I will undergo metamorphosis and be taken back to my School. I'll be safe and it's thanks to you."

"Anyway," said Dora. "Even if the Wirdegen had caught up with you again, you could have made that sound that drove them all away before."

"Audio defence?" said Bond. "No, Solita needs to recharge before she can be used for audio defence again. It would take a very long time to recharge here using sunlight alone."

Lewis started as if in surprise, then his head tilted back almost as if some invisible hand was forcing his chin back against his will. "Bond," he said in a strange voice. As he spoke, the quivering they had begun to recognize and fear started again, very faintly at first, but becoming stronger. The world strummed like a quavering musical note and the air, already tormented with shifting time, was seeded with black points. Lewis cried out flinging himself around wildly as if struggling with an invisible assailant. He twisted and panted then suddenly screamed out, "Run, Bond! Run! They're coming to get you. They made me listen! I couldn't help it. They know you can't break them up anymore."

"Maintain elementary Chikkulen breathing," commanded Solita in the voice of the School. Around them the black points deepened once more into holes burnt in the air, then stretched and began to take on the vague shape of men. To her astonishment, Jake saw Bond standing passively, staring as if hypnotized by the appearances in front of them.

"Run!" she yelled at him, waving the stick. "Run, Bond. Dora – get him out of here. Make him run in the right direction." Her tone carried an urgency that made Dora automatically obey. She seized Bond's right hand, Lewis took the left, and they hurried him along the bed of the stream between the narrow banks. Jake's fingers tightened around her stick. "Run!" she screamed again.

"What about you? What will you do?" Dora cried back, panic-stricken, retreating obediently despite her anxiety for Jake.

"I'm okay," Jake replied. She was being swept

along by a storybook idea but there seemed no other choice. Every moment they gained meant something real to Bond, a little more time in which to return to his School.

"Jake!" called Dora, "Come on!"

"Just get Bond out of here!" bellowed Jake. "I've got the stick."

Now the quivering became a convulsion. The world twisted and writhed beneath Jake's feet. Jake was flung from side to side and rolled over and over. All light began to flow out of the world as if a plug had been pulled out somewhere letting all the brightness drain away. She fell against the rocky wall — but it was rock no longer. It grew soft and vanished under the impact of her shoulder. The black shapes before her were also changed. They became white shapes and Jake felt as if she was inside a camera, living in a photographic film where light and dark were reversed.

"You can't hold us off with sticks," a voice scoffed. It was one of three people now confronting her. He had a shock of hair that was probably white in real life, and glaring yellow eyes with the pupil running across the eye, not vertically as in a cat's eye.

"Bond?" asked one of the others.

"Gone!" Jake replied, brandishing her stick in front of her as if it was a sword. "He's gone!"

"Go too!" cried the goatish man. "Run after him." All at once Jake realized that the longer she kept talking, the more time Bond might have, wherever he had gone.

"I have to take care of people," she began, waving her stick madly and babbling at these unnatural beings. "At home I look after my mother and my grandparents. I cook and I work the chainsaw to cut the wood. It's become a habit to me now. I'm looking after Bond. I'm looking after Dora and Lewis. I'm ... "

The man took a pace towards her and Jake struck at him with her stick. Where it touched him it burst into flames causing the nerves in her arm to jump wildly so that her whole arm jerked upwards, holding the stick aloft like a flaming torch. As the light of the fire fell on her opponents she thought at first that they were not very different from ordinary men – then saw with shock and despair that they did have vital differences. They had wings. Bond had not mentioned this.

"He's not here," said one, "we're wasting our time." They rose and swept past her like a storm cloud. The flame flared and then was extinguished. In the darkness Jake felt them all go by but there was nothing she could do to stop them. They did not hurt her, but she cowered below them as if they were a storm of knives which might cut her to pieces. She had done all she could, and had been defeated as she had known she must be. Now she was entitled to rest, or that was how it seemed to her as she lay in the dark. Then she found herself wondering where the trees were – where the stream had gone. Time had jolted again and this time she was completely lost in it. Something moved in the dark.

Jake went stiff with a different fear. Something stepped and snorted beside her and she felt a hairy serpent fall out of the air, twisting over her chest and across her face. It was followed by a velvety touch, and hot breath. Her nose was filled with a scent she recognized but could not immediately name.

A moment later she knew what it was. There was a horse standing beside her in the dark. The hairy serpent was only a tethering rope. Jake screwed up her eyes tightly waiting for the horse to tread on her. Instead it made a faint whickering sound. It was pleased to find a friend. Slowly Jake sat up and took hold of the rope. She pulled herself to her feet, and began clumsily to pat the horse's neck and sides. It was saddled and bridled but the bit was out of its mouth and the stirrups were hitched up. She could not yet see it, although other shapes were gradually becoming visible, outlined in silver, evidence that they belonged to another time from her own. *Lost in time,* chanted a voice in her mind, but she ignored it. She had had Bond and Lewis and Dora to look after, and now she had a horse too. It seemed too much. Holding the rope in one hand, feeling the way ahead with what was left of the smouldering stick, Jake began to move on again but in the dark she had no direction.

"Dora!" she called aloud but there was no reply. Not that she really expected there would be. Earlier they had used the stream to guide them but now Jake could not find anything to follow. Sometimes she stood still, feeling the horse snort

anxiously down her neck as she waved the glowing
stick in front of her. She knew it must be one of the
Rackham horses but which one she was unable to
tell. After a while she moved on again – and
walked straight into a rock, striking her knee with
the sort of bang that hurts like an electric shock.
Once again all her nerves seemed to jump in
sympathy, and she felt slightly nauseous.
Crouching down by the rock she rested her forehead against it, her face contorted with pain.

After a while as the pain subsided, a thought
came to her. She had banged her knee on an edge.
The rock was knee-high and flattish on the top. She
manoeuvred the horse as best she could, and
realized that it was not quite as dark as it had been
a moment ago. When the horse moved its head she
could actually see it as a silver outline against the
night. Jake raised her eyes. There was a red light,
faint but angry, up in the air which made her
wonder if the sun could possibly be rising from
behind unseen hills. Feeling her way gingerly, inch
by inch, Jake climbed onto the rock and threw
herself across the horse's back.

"I can't ride," she told it, "so please be good." It
moved nervously as she kicked and scrambled
herself into a seated position in the saddle, a
surprise for her horse-riding muscles which thought
they had finished for the day. Once up on the
horse, Jake could see something she could not have
seen before – another patch of light, whiter and
more like a street lamp than the red glow overhead. While she stared at it the horse put its ears

forward and edged towards it, so that she glimpsed the shape of its head again. There was something familiar about its ears, but one pair of horse's ears probably looked very like another. As they came closer and closer to the white light, Jake began to make out first shapes and then people. She could not see Bond, but she had found Dora and Lewis — and found them in terrifying company.

15. The Three Stones

When the sudden darkness fell, Dora, Bond and Lewis had struggled around a bend of the creek bed and were hurrying on as fast as they could.

Solita, bumping at Bond's side as he ran, continued to reel off numbers and co-ordinates. Bond could not possibly be taking note of them thought Dora, but she was quite wrong. He could listen and remember even as he ran. The mathematical instructions being relayed to him were like a set of building blocks, and by using the ideas they held he was able to make a structure which began to form a definite pattern. As he ran, the pattern affected him. He could feel his bones contracting and felt a change come upon him.

"I must stop," he said despairingly. To be so close to being rescued by the School and then to be caught by the Wirdegen seemed a bitter blow, but he knew he could not carry on during his metamorphosis.

"Hide!" commanded Dora, as she stopped and clasped her hand dramatically to her side as though she had been shot or had the stitch. In truth she was perfectly all right — out of breath perhaps, but able to run further if she needed to. "Hide behind those bushes and Lewis and I will guard you." It was then that the darkness came, and the world pitched like a ship at sea. "Oh dear," sobbed Dora. "Oh dear, oh dear." She continued saying this until everything grew still once more. "Where are we?" she cried aloud.

Lewis answered from so closely beside her that he took her by surprise. "It's stopped," he stated. "Was it an earthquake?"

"A time quake," Dora replied, but the thought of it made her feel even worse. There was a little light coming from somewhere. It was Solita still whispering and shining faintly in the dark.

"The stream's gone," said Lewis in a small voice. "We've gone back a million years."

"We'll have to be real eagles. They used to be here a million years ago," said Dora. She blindly drew him close to give him a comforting hug, misjudging his whereabouts in the dark and banging her nose on his ear.

"We've left Jake behind with only a stick to defend herself," said Lewis.

"It was my fault. But she made us go."

"How could it be your fault, silly?" asked Dora.

"Because of the spy hiding in my head," Lewis replied. "He looked out through my eyes and listened with my ears. He called the others and I couldn't stop him!"

Before Dora had time to think about this or do more than squeeze Lewis's hands reassuringly, there was a breathy roar in the air. They were no longer alone. Dora promptly ducked her head down with her arms wrapped across it as though she feared something might fall from above into her hair, but in actual fact she was trying to squeeze herself down so small that no-one would notice her. "Go away!" she cried in a muffled voice. "He's not here."

"Bond!" said a voice, and at the same time the stone around Dora's neck began to burn and tug as if she was a compass and the stone was the needle trying to point to a secret north of its own.

"Show yourself, Bond!" demanded another voice, then all around them the dark began to wail with voices calling "Bond, Bond, Bond" until it sounded as if they were beseiged by a tribe of hundreds. All Lewis and Dora could do was clutch each other and stare up at their enemies. The sky had begun to redden a little. Light was coming from somewhere.

"We don't want to hurt you, Bond," said the first voice loudly, "but unless you deliver yourself to us, we will feel free to hurt your friends who are crouching at our feet."

Bond was not far away. Unlike Dora and Lewis, he could see in the dark. He knew that the stream and trees had vanished, and that they were now in a world of stone facing the hills over which they had ridden earlier but in a much more stark and jagged form. He also knew that in another few minutes the structure of numbers he had been given and the Xu formula would come together and the School would be able to put out a wave keyed to this particular pattern which he could follow back through the layers of the atmosphere, through space, to the waiting School. He gripped the Companion tightly. But Dora and Lewis remained at the feet of the Wirdegen.

"Solita," he said. "If I go to help them, can you – can you destroy me if – if you need to. I can't leave them, but neither must I allow myself to be used by the Wirdegen."

"Destroy?" Solita repeated. The mechanical voice sounded different, unexpectedly alive and emotional. "Destroy . . . "

"Quickly!" Bond snapped. "Before I have time to reconsider."

"I can destroy," Solita said faintly.

"Wait until I give the word," Bond ordered as he walked into the faint circle of radiance cast by his pursuers. Dora would not have recognized him had it not been for one thing – the blazing kiss-of-fire hair. Bond had changed shape and colour, but the kiss-of-fire hair burnt on relentlessly. The Bond who stood before them now appeared as a slim, winged creature whose neck was covered with lacy scallops – no longer beautiful, no longer familiar, but still the essence of a friend.

"Let them go," he said firmly. "Let them walk away. They're only accidental friends." As he spoke his image seemed to change still further. He was altering continually.

"You said there were no accidents," Dora cried rather incoherently. "You said it was all a pattern."

Bond turned his flaming head to catch her words. The stone burned at the base of her throat looking as if it was emitting light, and there on Bond's chest shone his own stone, restored to him once more. The light increased as if the two stones, neither of them now in their true time, were trying to add something to the argument. The air trembled around them.

The goatish man sighed, apparently with relief. He put his hand on Bond's shoulder; a hand which had longer fingers than a hand ought to have. "Come with us now, Bond!" he said triumphantly. "Confess yourself a victim. You no longer look anything like a hero." Bond's altered face, with his huge eyes and flat nose, turned towards the speaker so suddenly that Dora thought he had been surprised by something, though she could no longer read his expression.

"How did *you* know I wanted to look like a hero?" Bond asked slowly and quietly.

"You are trying to waste time," the man said, "but we know that within a few more moments you could simply dissolve away back to your School leaving us empty-handed. Take him away."

But within the next few minutes everything changed.

The first thing that happened was that Jake charged at them out of the night riding Cooney and looking even more like the Lone Ranger without her cowboy hat than she had ever looked with it. She clung to Cooney's mane with one hand letting the reins hang loosely about his neck, while with the other hand she swung the tethering rope as if it was a lasso, making straight for Bond and his captor. Caught unawares the goatish man looked up and released his grip on Bond who quickly moved away from him. Cooney shied one way, and Jake fell in the opposite direction tumbling down to land flat on her back at Bond's feet, while Cooney trotted a few steps away then stopped and looked back as if expecting praise and a treat of apples.

"Stay away from us," Bond shouted at the goatish man. "If I say the word my Companion here will destroy me. None of us can win." At these words Bond's enemies turned towards him, and Dora thought they looked afraid. "Besides," continued Bond, "all this — it's been part of the test, hasn't it?"

There was a brief silence. "Part of the test?" repeated one of the enemies.

"When I left the School my teacher was the only one who knew I wanted to look like a hero. It was a joke — but you must have come from the School to know about it," he announced, half jubilantly, half angrily.

Jake picked herself up, looking at Bond incredulously. Dora voiced her thoughts. "You mean they're your *friends?*" she cried in disbelief, while Bond and his opponents stared steadily at each other. It was Solita who spoke.

"Notice of threat!" she said. "Major object anomaly is imminent." Even as she said this there was a flare of new light. Off to Dora's right three young men had come out of the darkness and now stood shielding their eyes, dazzled and amazed at the scene before them. Two were dark and one was fair, yet they were dressed alike in a mixture of traditional Maori and European clothes.

Historical men, thought Dora, for they reminded her of pictures from a history book. Outlined in broad bands of silver light they stood there, lips moving, obviously talking to one another although no sound reached the group standing around Bond. A fantastic possibility flashed into Dora's mind. She saw with amazement that the fair man wore an identical stone in his ear to that which hung around her own neck, the same stone that hung around Bond's neck like a worn splinter of green.

A moment later she felt as if she had been seized in a soft but unyielding vice. The air grew solid about her as though she had been set in glowing glass. Bond, already in his true shape, did not change dramatically but his 'opponents' did. Sprouting upwards like columns of light they became patterns in which remarkable shapes moved, looking sometimes like faces, sometimes like birds, and sometimes like the letters of an unknown alphabet. Fixed as they were, Jake, Lewis and Dora could all see each other. Some time later, Dora would think that that was the moment she began to lose her fear of never looking good enough, but all she could think of now was that Jake looked beautiful and human, and she could tell that Jake was thinking the same thing about her. In spite of their differences, they were inhabitants of the same planet after all.

Hanging from Bond's shoulder, Solita was the only one able to speak. "We shall now return to the School," she said. The columns of light all moved together, melted into one another and became one, widening to engulf Bond who stood set in their light like a red-headed goblin caught in a rod of amber. The stone around his neck glowed in a ghostly fashion. It glowed in the ear of the fair historical man, and Dora felt it burn her own skin.

The children were surprised when Solita addressed them in their own language. "Bond will be safe," reported Solita. "I speak with the voice of the School. You have fallen under the power of a dislocation field brought about by the simultaneous presence of one object in three different times. It has created what we call a local paradox. As Bond returns to his School there will be another jump in time and you will all be set free. You must then be patient and in due course your own time will reassert itself. Bond's memories of you will be recorded. You will become part of the Galgonquan Inventory. But now we must resolve this knot and say goodbye. Thank you. You have been brave friends."

Solita began to emit a sound which was like nothing the three children had ever heard before. It was musical and soft, but seemed to go right through them as though their very bones had become harp strings. Its effect on the Galgonqua was stranger still. Their colours left them. They grew transparent, a tall column of glass. In the last second Bond half turned towards them and his lips moved, but no words came, only a faint, far-off murmur like the sound of the sea, and then they were gone. A door had shut. Bond was on one side of it and Jake, Dora and Lewis were on the other. There was a little jump – nowhere near as violent or frightening as the previous one. The light changed suddenly. They still stood in darkness, but were surrounded by a mysterious silver lace as if the world had become a puzzle of shining wire.

"The other men have gone too," remarked Lewis. "The Maoris."

"You know who it was, don't you?" Jake turned to Dora. "It was Sebastian Webster."

Dora had already worked this out but rebelled against the knowledge. "It can't have been," she cried.

"It was. It all fits in," said Jake. "The first jump by the waterfall took us back to Webster's time, and then the next one dragged him and his friends back with us. That was the earthquake. *We* were his vision – *we* were the mannikins!"

Dora knew Jake was right. She and Lewis and Jake and Cooney had been ghosts. Having always been frightened of the haunted valley, she now knew who it was that haunted it. It was herself she had been afraid of all the time.

The redness of the light increased around them. Jake lifted her gaze to the black mass beyond the point where the Galgonqua had stood. Now she could see that it was a mountain – more than a mountain. The ground purred strangely, then growled and shifted. As she looked, a deep, rosy flow erupted at the peak of the mountain in a dazzling fountain. The night became like Guy Fawkes night except that the fireworks let off on the fifth of November could not compare with the spectacle before them now. They were no longer on a peninsular but on an island. There was no longer any harbour beyond the hills, but an erupting volcano.

"What will we do?" asked Jake.

"Sit tight," suggested Dora. "It's what we were told to do." She looked around wildly. "Did you hear that?"

"What? The volcano?"

"No!" declared Dora, frowning. "Somebody called my name."

"They can't have," said Jake, but as she spoke she heard her own name called, faintly but distinctly.

"Ghosts!" Dora cried. "First men from outer space, then historical men, then a volcano, and now ghosts!" But it was not ghosts. It was David and Philippa coming out of the dark towards the light to find their children at last.

"It's Mum!" cried Lewis, forgetting the volcano and Bond too. "I knew we'd get home safely."

16. New Directions

Up in the School, Bond walked for the last time through the rounded corridor of the student's section. His friends were still asleep. He had been returned to the School at the exact moment at which he had left it two and a half days earlier.

"Nexus ahead," advised a soft, mechanical voice and the rosy cone of light deepened in front of him once more. He saw the chair and the screen and the moving worms of light. To his surprise he found that some of the dials which he had not understood previously had developed some meaning for him and he could not think how it was that he could recognize them. The screen lit up.

"Bond," said the voice of his teacher. "They tell me you passed the test – though not without difficulty and making several mistakes. I hear that you made contact with the ancestors and involved them in your test. You know that is forbidden and you are only forgiven because you recorded good information. The use of hair dye was of particular interest."

Bond did not reply.

"Are you pleased?" asked the teacher. "You are now a probationer and will be reunited with your sister Solita once more. They are presently waking and disconnecting her."

"I don't understand," said Bond, "why you would allow anyone to take over Lewis. He was so little and helpless."

"You were the one who made the contact," the teacher pointed out, "and all that happened to them was as a direct result of your involving them in your test. If the Wirdegen had really been after you, things might have been a great deal worse for them."

"If the Wirdegen had really been after me I would have been caught a lot sooner," Bond replied, his voice heavy. "It explains a great deal."

"Don't underrate yourself, Bond. It is the same with all you confident students – if you can't be heroes you want to be villains. You were brave, you thought quickly, and at the end you were prepared to sacrifice yourself for your friends and for the School. In the end, too, you guessed that it was all part of the test. Give yourself credit for this."

"They became my friends," Bond explained. "They had a lot of troubles of their own, but they still became my friends." Something else suddenly occurred to him. "There was an object anomaly," he exclaimed. "The first one was only a slight one, but the second was serious even though the prophecy circuits said I could take my stone down to the city. They must have been wrong."

"No, they were not wrong," answered the teacher. "But something very mysterious was involved and we have a team working on an analysis now. It may be that this particular anomaly changed the lives of everyone involved – even the men from the past – in an important and necessary way. And now, Bond, you must go."

"I'll do better next time," Bond stated confidently, "but —"

"Lewis will not suffer at all," the teacher reassured him. "There is no danger for any of them." The screen went dark. Bond got up and began to walk away. Silently the screen behind him lit up again. "Bond! You are going in the wrong direction," called the teacher. "You have passed your first test, remember. And Bond – the School is proud of you."

Bond stopped in his tracks. Slowly he began to smile. Then he turned and walked down the rounded corridor in the opposite direction towards another part of the school, and as he walked, light ran beside him like a faithful dog.

★   ★   ★

In the distant past of the planet below, Sebastian Webster spoke through the darkness that surrounded them and said, "I can smell the bush. It's going to be all right after all."

"I knew the valley was full of ghosts," said Koro. "Everyone knows, but I didn't think a *pakeha* would see them."

"He's got Maori eyes after all," said Hakiaha. "He sees in the Maori way."

The tension had eased between Sebastian and his Maori friends. Sebastian touched the stone in his ear and felt it cold and smooth, as if the hills had wept a stone tear. It had no more messages for him. "I told you – I don't build fences," he said. "I don't fence anyone out, and I don't fence myself in. Not like the others."

And there among the ferns he sat patiently with his friends and waited for morning to come, which it did – as magical as the bush, the hills and the old volcano, not because it was strange but because it was familiar. Although he welcomed it with Maori feelings, Sebastian also had one *pakeha* thought as the sunlight fell on him. *Someday*, he thought, *I'll write it all down*. He knew he could not quite tell it or sing it in the Maori way of passing information down through generations. It would have to be written. Then he rose and walked with his people down into the volcano which time had turned into a smooth, green harbour.

17. The Beginning Place

When Jake and Dora saw their parents, they understood at once that no matter how frightening the events of the last twenty minutes had seemed to them, it had been even worse for these grown-ups who had not known anything about Bond. Even explanations you were unable to understand were better than no explanations at all, and perhaps children, being closer to fairy tales, could cope better with terrifying transformations. So it was Dora and Jake and Lewis who did most of the comforting as well as the explaining, and Cooney who was probably the most at ease in this remarkable world in which they now found themselves.

However strange and unnatural things seemed, finding the children safe and well meant so much that it was not very long before Philippa and David stopped shaking with fear and shock and began to act like parents again – joking a little and refusing to take things too seriously in case the gravity of the situation got too much for them once more. At first they looked only at their children and not at the changed world around them, but soon they began to dart curious glances out into the darkness and up into the air and their voices grew softer and more normal again. Nevertheless they made everyone hold hands in case, by some unimaginable magic, one of them should be plucked away and lost forever.

The roar of the volcano filled the air and the sky above turned the colour of molten steel, but the patchwork family reunited at its foot did not particularly notice.

"There are things more important than volcanoes," said David grandly, and for a few moments it seemed that simply being together was enough to make a happy ending. But the volcano did not wish to be ignored. It had never had an audience until now, for it had risen out of the sea long before there were any people around and it wanted people to notice it and to tremble at its force.

"Noisy old thing!" commented David nervously, staring up at it. It painted his face with its savage light. "I don't think it can hurt us though. We seem to be untouchable here. I think if we were as close to a volcano in our own time, it would be deafening."

It was curious that they had wound up huddled together in a circle among the stones like jittery hens. They had started off hugging each other over and over again while Cooney, snorting scornfully and shifting his feet on the stones, watched them. From the children's point of view it was a wonderfully secure feeling to have parents around who might know what to do.

When Dora expressed this sentiment however, David replied, "But I don't know what to do! There's nothing in the Good Parent's Instruction Manual to tell you what to do when you're lost in time with a volcano as a next-door neighbour!" Nevertheless it was true that the relief of being together made the strangeness seem less so.

"I'm so glad to see you," Jake said to David, and cried big, wet, silent tears onto his shoulder, because she was speaking not just for that moment, but for yesterday and the day before that and the year before that. She was telling him in her own way that she had been frightened of riding, frightened of adventure, but mostly frightened of giving in.

"I was scared," admitted Dora. "Jake was the brave one."

"Dora was so brave," cried Jake simultaneously.

"I was too," Lewis said proudly. Their three voices made a pattern. They had started off as individuals from different planets but at last they were breathing the same air. Just for a moment Bond was forgotten.

"What's been going on, anyway?" asked David. "What have you done to the world?"

"We went back to the days of Sebastian Webster," said Lewis. "We had a turn at being ghosts." The mountain roared and great rivers of incandescent fire began to wind down its sides. They shone like great tears, destroying everything in their path. "It feels so old," Lewis sighed. "We went back in time with Bond and the ones that were after him."

"Bond!" Philippa cried in sudden recollection. "Where is he? I can't imagine what's happened to him."

"It isn't a thing you can imagine," explained Jake. "Bond wasn't a real person. He was something else, but he said we weren't to worry. He said time would go faster and faster until whole years went by in seconds and we would end up in our own time — exactly when we left it — and we'd go on from there."

"We'll wait then," said David, "because I for one don't want to find myself wandering too far away from where we left the horses. So — let's just sit here and talk about the weather!"

Lewis laughed at David's joke. "There isn't any weather here," he said. "No sun, nothing but the light of the volcano."

"But the sun's rising, I'm sure of it," Philippa said. "There's a glow in the sky over there — away from the volcano. I'm sure it's the beginning of a new day — or should I say an old one."

"An old, *old* one!" added Lewis.

They sat and watched for a while in silence. The sky began to change colour before their eyes. It was the most brilliant sunrise any of them could remember seeing. It looked as if the surface of the sky was polished and was reflecting the volcano's glow in pink and gold so brightly it seemed as if it might suddenly burst into flames and burn up overhead. When the sun did rise it moved so rapidly that Lewis felt an angel was drawing an arch over their heads with a felt pen that left a line of fire.

"It's so scary," said Philippa in wonderment, "and yet – look Dora – it's beautiful too, in a frightening way. Like a film that's been speeded up."

"I'm never going to be frightened of anything again," remarked Dora. "So many frightening things have happened today I've used up all my scaredness!"

They were in a barren world. Although there were a few trees, they looked distant and stunted. They were the only living things in a landscape of stone mottled with yellow sulphur. Steam rose from crevices in the flank of the mountain, and the air was filled with a burnt chemical smell.

"Isn't it funny," reflected Dora. "David wished we could get back to some beginning place and here we are!" She looked respectfully at David as if here was a man whose wishes, no matter how unlikely, had a chance of coming true.

"Yes, David, it's all your fault," said Philippa good-naturedly. Cooney, his lead rope tucked under a heavy stone so that he couldn't wander away, snorted as if he agreed.

"I actually rode him," said Jake to no-one in particular. "I stuck on for quite a while."

The sun moved faster and faster. "It's making me dizzy," complained Lewis. "I can see the shadows spinning around."

"It's true!" said Jake suddenly, but without saying what it was that was true. "Dora's still got the same hair of course, but it's very untidy . . . "

"I don't care," Dora butted in, touching her head anxiously all the same.

" . . . and I haven't got my cowboy hat," continued Jake. "Lewis hasn't got his felt pens or eagle feathers, and there's no new house and no red car."

"But we've got each other!" declared Philippa.

"That's right," David agreed. "Remember how we wished we'd get back to a place where there was nothing to hide behind, no props and no history? Then we'd be able to talk to each other, ask questions, give honest answers —"

"Okay," said Jake. "So why didn't you ask me to your wedding?" She directed a penetrating look at David who considered his reply carefully.

"Jacqueline – Jake," he said at last. "I *did* invite you. Your mother wrote back saying you didn't want to come. I had written a long, careful letter because I knew it might be awkward, even upsetting for you, but I wanted you to be there. I was very happy and wanted to share it with you if possible - but Pet said you didn't want to come."

"Oh," said Jake. It was her turn to be silent. Dora opened her mouth to say something but Philippa caught her eye and shook her head. "She reads the letters you write me," Jake said after a while. "She's frightened I might want to live with you for always and then there'd be no-one to look after things at home."

"Look after things?" asked Philippa, puzzled.

"Jake's grandma and grandpa aren't very well," said Dora, secretly pleased that she knew something her mother didn't, "and her mother wants to be looked after."

"It isn't her fault!" Jake cried defensively. "It's just that she never learned to look after herself, and slowly she grew more and more disappointed and can't see any reason to try hard."

"Do you have to do all the dishes?" asked Lewis, aghast at the thought. "Dry them too?"

"Uh-huh. I help cook and peel the veges and things like that," said Jake. "And I do the washing and cut the wood, and sometimes do a bit of gardening, and remember to put out the milk bottles, and dress my grandpa. I have to learn how to look after myself and it's all good practice."

"You should come and live with us forever," Lewis offered generously.

Jake looked at David. "I have a pretty good time in a lot of ways," she continued. "I have some good friends at school. And I know Mum really does love me even if she doesn't want to look after me the way other mothers look after their children."

"I know," David said in a gentle voice.

"She says that I need her, but really she needs me."

"I know," repeated David sadly.

"We have some good times. Sometimes she'll say, for no reason at all, 'Let's have a party!' and we do. It's a lot of fun but the trouble is we spend all the housekeeping and have to live on mince for a week. I still like things like that though."

"What if she marries Manley?" asked Dora.

"I think she's got too much sense for that," Jake replied. "I mean she knows Manley would never look after anyone but she likes having someone to go to the movies with. They go to films that I'm not allowed into."

A rapid night fell over them. They sat quietly watching as the stars moved like glittering moths blown over the sky by a high wind.

"The thing with me," said Dora, encouraged by Jake's disclosures, "is that I'm always afraid someone will come in when I'm not expecting it and catch me out looking awful, and then he'll go away again."

"Your father perhaps?" asked David, probingly.

"I don't know," said Dora looking puzzled. "Sometimes, perhaps. Not that I want you to go away, David," she added quickly.

They could all see David's funny, sad smile by the light of the volcano. "We can all tell a secret or two at the beginning of the world," he said. "Life's very mixed up, Dora. It's just the way it is. There's no need to worry too much about it. There are times when your mother misses your father too."

"Yes, every now and then something happens which I think is funny but David takes it so seriously," said Philippa. "I don't exactly miss Joe at times like that but I do think of him because I know he would have thought it was funny too. And every now and then David thinks of Jake's mother in the same way."

"Mmm. Like, as Jake was saying, sometimes Pet would say 'Let's have a party!' and she'd spend all the housekeeping," said David. "And we had some wonderful parties. Even if we did have to live on mince for a fortnight. It's hard to say these things under a family roof, but it's different under a volcano."

The days and nights shivered around them. Months and years flickered by. Whole summers went past like the flashes of a distant mirror. The volcano climbed higher while they watched, then it grew darker and slower.

Rain and frost worked on it but the small family group were not touched by wetness or by cold. The crater began to crumble at its upper edges and at last everything ran into a strange twilight just as Bond had predicted – no sun, no moon, no day, no night – only their five faces looking at each other and the nervous stamp of Cooney's hooves on the stones.

"You'll be able to learn to ride when we get back," said Dora, already imagining herself teaching Jake to ride and how grateful Jake would be to her forever after, and somehow this thought turned into a dream. She sighed, leaned against David and closed her eyes. "I'll never throw books at Jake again," she promised drowsily.

"Even if you do, I suppose we'll get over it sooner or later," Jake said smiling, but Dora did not hear her. She was asleep.

"Don't you believe in happy endings?" David asked his daughter.

"I suppose I do," replied Jake yawning. "Sort of. For a while anyway!" She lay back against Philippa. "Do you think this is a happy ending?"

"It's hard to say," David answered. "Funnily enough, I do feel happy, but I'm not sure if it's an ending or a beginning."

"Maybe it's both," said Philippa wisely. "A circle."

Each one of them gradually drifted off to sleep, Dora and Lewis snuggled up to David, and Jake leaning against Philippa. When at last they awoke, they opened their eyes to a world of dappled shadows and patches of sky seen through green leaves.

"This is where we started from," said David. "Let's see if we can find the rest of our poor horses."

The creek flowed along murmuring to itself. It sounded as if it had always been there and always would be. It was hard to imagine a time when there had been no creek, and no trees, only stones. A time when the ridges of the eastern hills had glowed and overflowed with the burning gold of molten rock. Yet the land had made itself before their eyes.

The five people and a horse wandered along the creek bed until they came upon a place where they saw, with astonishment, their own footprints on the bank of the creek. They scrambled up the slope with Cooney following them obediently, and found all the other horses standing quietly on the open ridge that overlooked Webster's Bush. Cooney flicked his tail and went to join them.

At the sight of the horses David stopped, perplexed. "One horse too many!" he exclaimed, then frowned. "Wasn't there someone else with us?" he asked vaguely.

Philippa and Dora looked at each other, puzzled. Jake was silent.

"I think there was," Lewis said. "A sort of brightly-coloured person." He looked around as if expecting a brightly-coloured person to step out of the clear air of the valley.

"I think he went the long way home," said Jake, half remembering. "He met friends unexpectedly and went home with them instead."

"We'll have to lead the extra horse," Philippa said. "It's just as well they know me at the riding school."

"I'll lead it," volunteered Jake. "But go slowly, so that I can get a bit more used to the feeling of Cooney."

"If you want to practise trotting, I'll take a turn," Dora offered generously. "It's funny, though! I have the feeling that everything's changed, yet when I look around everything's the same."

"I think things have changed," commented Jake, "but I don't mind. They're better than they were before."

"He was a sort of eagle," Lewis said, still looking around, "and then he flew off." But he no longer remembered quite whom he was talking about. His memory was crowded with images of trees growing, volcanoes spouting fire, and years flickering by like pages swiftly turning. His head felt as if it was filled with dreams – but then it often felt like that.

"The extra horse can be a packhorse," Philippa said, putting the pack with the lunch and the spare jackets and other necessary things over Scoot's back.

"He went the long way home," Jake repeated, frowning as if she was trying hard to remember more, "but he didn't need to stay any longer."

Nobody heard her.

ABOUT THE AUTHOR

Margaret Mahy is New Zealand's premiere author of books for children and young adults. She has twice won Britain's prestigious Carnegie Medal, for *The Haunting* in 1982 and *The Changeover: A Supernatural Romance* in 1984 (both of which are available in Scholastic paperback editions). *The Changeover* was also named a YASD Best Book for Young Adults, an ALA Notable Children's Book, a *School Library Journal* Best Book, and a *Horn Book* Fanfare List Book.

Before becoming a full-time writer, Margaret Mahy was a children's librarian in New Zealand, where she has lived all her life. She is the author of dozens of picture books for younger readers, and of *The Catalogue of the Universe*, a young adult novel that has been published recently. Margaret Mahy lives outside Christchurch, New Zealand.

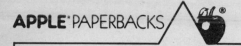

APPLE®PAPERBACKS

For Ages 11-13...
A New Kind of Apple Filled with Mystery, Adventure, Drama, and Fun!

$2.25 U.S./$2.95 CAN.

- ☐ 33024-1 **Adorable Sunday** Marlene Fanta Shyer
- ☐ 40174-2 **Welcome Home, Jellybean** Marlene Fanta Shyer
- ☐ 33822-6 **The Alfred Summer** Jan Slepian
- ☐ 40168-8 **Between Friends** Sheila Garrigue
- ☐ 32192-7 **Blaze** Robert Somerlott
- ☐ 33844-7 **Frank and Stein and Me** Kin Platt
- ☐ 33558-8 **Friends Are Like That** Patricia Hermes
- ☐ 32818-2 **A Season of Secrets** Alison Cragin Herzig and Jane Lawrence Mali
- ☐ 33797-1 **Starstruck** Marisa Gioffre
- ☐ 32198-6 **Starting with Melodie** Susan Beth Pfeffer
- ☐ 32529-9 **Truth or Dare** Susan Beth Pfeffer
- ☐ 32870-0 **The Trouble with Soap** Margery Cuyler
- ☐ 40128-9 **Two-Minute Mysteries** Donald J. Sobol
- ☐ 40129-7 **More Two-Minute Mysteries** Donald J. Sobol
- ☐ 40130-0 **Still More Two-Minute Mysteries** Donald J. Sobol
- ☐ 40054-1 **A, My Name Is Ami (For Girls Only)** Norma Fox Mazer
- ☐ 40352-4 **Our Man Weston** Gordon Korman
- ☐ 33593-6 **The Phantom Film Crew** Nancy K. Robinson

Scholastic Inc.
P.O. Box 7502, 2932 East McCarty Street, Jefferson City, MO 65102

Please send me the books I have checked above. I am enclosing $_____
(please add $1.00 to cover shipping and handling). Send check or money order—no cash or C.O.D.'s please.

Name_____

Address_____

City_____State/Zip_____
Please allow four to six weeks for delivery. Offer good in U.S.A. only. Sorry, mail order not available to residents of Canada.

AMM861

Get ready for friends...
Get ready for fun...
Get ready for...

JUNIOR HIGH

Get ready for a fresh new year of 8th grade madness at Cedar Groves Junior High! Laugh at best friends Nora and Jen's "cool" attempts to fit in. Cringe at the exceptionally gross tricks of Jason, the class nerd. Be awed by Mia who shows up on the first day dressed in a punk outfit. And meet Denise, "Miss Sophistication," who shocks Nora and Jen by suggesting they invite *BOYS* to the Halloween party!

Get ready for **JUNIOR HIGH,** a new series about the funny side of life in junior high school.